The Lady or the Tiger, Death Mask and Eulogy, and Other Re-Imaginings

J. M. McDermott

TO ANGELA

CONTENTS

DEATH MASK AND EULOGY

The street crier threw pebbles at
Nova Coates' window for a penny a
week to wake him up just before
dog hour. Nova was already
awake, lying in bed and waiting.
Nova stared at a bottle of
laudanum on his dresser. He heard
more pebbles on the glass. He
wondered if he could find a way to
sleep through his work day, and go
straight to the tavern, and his
friends, there – Yolanda, Melissa,
and all the painters and the poets.

His father's death mask glowed
like a candle on the wall. His
painted eyes watched Nova with
sorrow.

Laudanum first, then food, then
wine. Marducci had already left for
his shift, at the gates. Nova felt
Marducci's side of the bed for any
residual heat. There was none.
He'd been gone for hours.
Marducci must have waited for
Nova to fall asleep before leaving.

Nova ate his fill of bread, cheese
and dried meats every time he
woke up. If he carried any food
underground, the orphans would
steal it. He risked carrying two
flasks of watered-down brandy
mixed with laudanum inside his
cloak. He moved them around
among his pockets, to throw off the
little thieves but he still lost a
flask to their fingers every few
weeks.

Nova's tools of office were piled on
the floor in a heap. First, Nova
pulled up a huge cape – filthy, now
- with a noble family's seal, like a
flag draped across his shoulders.
Second, Nova picked up a large
ash staff, hooked like a shepherd's
to hold the lamp. Third, he picked
up two lamps, one hanging from
the staff and lit. The other hung
from a rope at his belt, unlit, in
case the first lamp burned down.

Nova sat down on a chair. He took
another long drink of laudanum.
He looked up at his father's death
mask. He spoke to it, as if it could
hear him speaking. It could not.
"Father, I wish Yolanda had

2

painted you a face that looked
happy, father. She says that
unscrupulous artists will do that,
sometimes, because it makes the
families happy. I wish you had
been happier."

Nova's neighbors were all asleep in
their tiny rooms. More pebbles
came for the window. The crier
didn't know if Nova was awake or
not. Outside, in the street, Nova
and the crier greeted each other
silently. Nova threw a penny at
the crier that had thrown rocks.
She shouted something at him, but
Nova wasn't really listening. Nova
said, "Did you say something?"

"Funeral today," she said. "Best
hurry."

"Who?"

"Some noble kid. Thought she was
a Caligari."

"Mine?"

"Maybe. They don't announce

suicides."

Nova jogged quickly over to the crier and pressed another coin into her palm. She winked at him, and flipped the coin into her mouth. She sucked on it like candy. She wandered off into the poor neighborhoods pressed against the city wall. She dragged out her shout, "D-O-O-O-OG HOUR! N-O-O-O NEWS!"

Nova ran until he reached the funeral at the night gate of the city wall. He wished the crier had gotten to his window sooner. He looked for a family crest, but he saw none. No one wore crests for a suicide. Phosphorous was smeared all over their skin and clothes, an ethereal and unearthly green light in all that darkness and lamplight. They marched solemnly. If the corpse had died naturally, they'd be pounding drums in evening twilight and waving flags with her family's crest, weeping loudly – paying undertaker's wives to weep for days. Suicides were buried quietly at dog hour, in shame.

Nova would have difficulty remembering the name of his master. It had been at least a year since he had thought enough of the unseen employer to recall anything about his work but the place he had to go every night, and the overseer that came by with lamp oil and money without bothering about the master's name. Three years ago, Nova met his employer, but it was only once and the man had looked Nova up and down like he was buying a horse instead of a tomb guard. The noble's name, to Nova, was only a sigil in the dark on a cape he wore every day when no one was around to respect it. The ones who worked with the dead around Nova had little patience for social graces among the painted masks, the eulogies, meat and bones.

The mourners in the street were for a noble. This night's ceremony was large enough for a full funeral. There were even priests. The priests would have to be bribed to get them out for a suicide in the middle of the night.

Nova couldn't politely push his way past the procession. Nova had to slip out a side gate, where his lover, Marducci, worked the night shift. He and Nova embraced, quickly, in the dark where no one would see them. They kissed.

"You smell terrible, Nova. Worse than a field surgeon. You need a bath. You need twelve baths, one after another, and a better job that doesn't smell so bad."

"I need your help, Marducci."

"Anything, my love."

"Sneak me out at the side gate, quickly."

Marducci did not hesitate. He unlocked the gate – a crime to do that at this gate after dark – and quickly Nova slipped out into the outer city.

It had rained today. Running through mud was loud and difficult. Nova worried he'd interrupt the ceremony.

Nova got to the catacombs in time,
with the luminous procession still
marching down the hills from the
city wall, like a giant caterpillar
smeared in firefly blood.

Nova stepped into the mouth of the
cave and walked carefully over the
bricks. Orphans slept in rags,
anywhere they fell. Nova didn't
want to trip over any of them,
wake them up, and hear their
begging for coins and clothes.

The first thing he heard on the job,
after he was given his supplies,
was that he was never, ever to give
a single thing – even if it was
worthless – to the orphans. He was
never to let any of them into the
tombs, for any reason, and if he
saw one entering another family's
tomb he was to try and stop them
if he could without being very late.

There were other guards with
other families, but all the paths
twisted below the hills, and few of

them ever met in the dark, or on the way through the dark.

Nova got to the tomb where he worked at night, sitting in the solid ash doorway. He waved at the man there before him.

"Hey, Pietro!" said Nova. "Suicide coming. Noble girl. Maybe ours."

"Oh, what a shame. Know anything?"

"Nothing. You'd best get moving. You'll be stuck here half the hour."

Pietro had only one hand. The other had been buried on a battlefield, decades back. He had a huge scar running from his white hair to his chin. Pietro had been guarding tombs long before Nova was born. Pietro smiled a lot, for no reason. He talked a lot, too. He talked about the different suicides he had seen here, about how he had to beat back hedge wizards once. They had wanted the body of a young woman who had killed herself, and Pietro had waved back their amateurish sorceries with

just the ash staff and lilac oil fire
like in the holy books.

Nova didn't believe any of it.

Nova nodded. Nova wasn't
listening.

Pietro was still talking.

Nova nodded, again, and wondered
why the orphans truly seemed to
avoid the man. Melissa had been
an orphan here, and she had said
that all the orphans feared Pietro
more than wizards – why, she
couldn't say. Nova also thought
about the other fellow that came
here, at the end of Nova's shift.
Nova didn't know that other
fellow's name. That one never
spoke. Nova liked the other fellow
better.

Pietro seemed to be waiting for a
response. Nova nodded, again. He
coughed and looked down the hall.

The phosphorous illumination
flickered on the wall. They weren't

here yet, but they were going to be here any moment. Nova stood up, at attention. Pietro turned mid-sentence to see the priest with two torches pacing forward in the dark. Pietro stiffened into a silent salute.

The dead woman was carried just behind the priests. She was wrapped in white linen and painted in glowing limes and phosphorous. She looked like a ghost. The men that carried her were grim as executioners. Her father held up her right shoulder at the head of the procession, where only a father or a husband or an eldest son ever stood. He was older than the other men, and shorter. He had a swaying gut like a sack. He had small eyes, with tear stains cutting through the paint along his cheeks.

Nova caught the man's eyes. Nova blinked and looked quickly away. He realized that he had recognized the old man, and it took a few moments to recall why.

The man was Nova's employer. Nova had only seen him once from

across a room, when the old man
had done a cursory inspection of
the new hires. Since then, Nova
had only ever seen his overseer
and fellow tomb guards.

The procession stopped at the door.
Now, Nova and his employer were
close enough to smell each other.
The thick myrrh of the dead
daughter coated the old man's
hands. It smelled thick as rotten
stew. Nova waited, at attention.
He tried not to blink, or breathe
too deep, or make any sort of noise.

Nova couldn't see the ceremony.

A priest painted green-glowing
runes around the doorknob. He
plucked the keys from Nova's belt.
He opened the ash door just a
crack at first, and released a bag of
fireflies into the darkness, ahead
of the procession, to light the
hallway. The priest threw lilac
flowers on the ground. He opened
the door completely. He bowed to
the darkness, and waved an ash
torch in the shape of the runes.

Nova held very still. He looked
through the bones and the stones
and through the trees of the
hillside around the catacombs,
past the wall and through the
houses, to the tavern at the end of
his day, where he would drink to
this death with the undertakers,
the eulogy poets, and the death
mask painters and all his friends
that were pariahs to society
because they worked among
cadavers.

The dead girl was placed on the
floor just inside the tomb, upon the
lilac flower, and she was left there.
The door closed behind her. Holy
runes were painted on the door in
phosphorous paint to discourage
wizards. Had she died honorably,
without sin, she would have been
placed deep inside the old tomb,
that ran for at least a mile through
these caves past Nova's door. As a
suicide, she was just barely worth
enough to her family to distract
the rats from the other bones. Still,
she was handled with care and
people had come to see her off.
Religion couldn't make anyone

stop caring about their lost girls.

2

When young women died, people tried to get to the body. Pietro had warned Nova about it, soon after the procession had gone. "Noble young women, especially virgins, and the suicide only sweetened the prize. Her soul's stuck in that pretty skin. Could be a wizard, a rival family, or some kind of pervert, but they're coming after the body until it starts to stink of rot. For a few days, carry a knife in your sleeve, just in case, and maybe a matchlock primed and dry if you have any. Do you have a matchlock?"

Nova held out his hand and closed it into a fist around the shaft of his staff. "Weapons are illegal. I've got this. It's sturdier than swords I've carried."

Pietro handed his ash staff to Nova to hold. He had only one hand, and needed it free to manipulate something under his cloak. Pietro pulled out an axe he had hidden, lashed under his shirt. Pietro silently reached under Nova's cloak, to give it to Nova. The axe slipped through Nova's belt loop, and dangled like a wicked tail.

"Give it back to me tomorrow," said Pietro. "I've got a spare."

Pietro took back his staff with his only hand. He left, whistling happily, as if a girl hadn't been buried tonight, as if he hadn't just handed an illegal weapon to Nova as casually as a drink of water.

Nova pulled out the axe when Pietro was gone. It had been years since he had touched a real weapon. This one was good, too. It was well-kept and sharp and the head was bolted solid into the clean shaft. Nova had a new story to give to Yolanda, and Melissa, and Marducci, and all the others, when he went to the tavern at the end of his night.

No one came to disturb the corpse.

Not even the orphans stirred to
heckle Nova over the dead.
After a long, quiet shift, the next
guard came to relieve Nova. This
guard was another old soldier, but
he never spoke or looked anyone in
the eye. Nova didn't know the
man's name. The man walked like
he was already carrying weapons,
and didn't need the axe. He sat
down, with neither a hello nor a
good-bye. He stared at the wall in
front of him. He pulled out his
flask and sipped, silently.

Nova told the sullen man that a
young woman had been buried in
the tomb - a suicide. The man
grunted.

Nova left. Outside, the sun
trembled just below the horizon.
Nova didn't need the lamp to see in
the dark. He walked into the main
gate, where early farmers
wandered to the market below the
cathedral. Nova reeked of the
catacombs. He smelled like lime,
rat feces, bone dust, and rot. Not
even prostitutes would touch him.

He was unclean.

He went to the only tavern in town that reveled in death, and his friends there, the revelers, where poets were already drunk and shouting in the early dawn.

3

"Take the ash staff when you travel dark roads! Carry garlic wreaths and a sigil of the woad..."

"You're stealing from Caligari, Muskrin! I've heard that before."

"Everyone steals the refrain from Caligari. It is the highest form of respect."

"Does your patron know anything about Caligari? Does he care that you're stealing from a true master and selling it like it is special and new and just for his mother's funeral?"

"My patron doesn't know poetry from a prostitute's ass. I borrow the brilliant refrain from Caligari, as many of you do, as a sign of respect. Now, let me finish. Take the ash staff when you travel dark roads. Carry garlic wreaths and a sigil of the woads. Marigolds for lovers and lilacs for disasters..." Then, all poets heckled all poets, all at the top of their large lungs. Nova pushed his way through the crowd of them. He squinted in the heavy candle-light to the bar of the tavern, searching for friends.

Yolanda was still there, necking with Melissa - a much younger woman - in the middle of the bar. Stools had emptied out next to them. People averted their eyes from the two women, loopy drunk from a long night of drinking, and shamelessly necking in the middle of the room like a boy and a girl in love. They could be arrested for it, but among these dead, perversion was not an important thing. Marducci had even kissed Nova here, once. He wasn't around.

Nova sat down loudly in the empty seat beside Yolanda. He stomped his hand on the counter. "Wine

and stew for a working man, Viri!
I'm the only fellow here with
steady coin! And wine for my
friends, Yolanda and Melissa, who
saved me my seat!"

Viri placed the thin wine, pink as a
watercolor, in front of the two
women. Viri put out lentil soup in
a mug, beside the heavily-watered
wine. Nova drank it all in big,
greedy gulps until the worst of his
hunger subsided. He felt the illegal
axe under his cloak, pushing into
his back every time he leaned back
to swallow. Nova drank more wine.
He waited. He listened to the poets
heckling each other, all of them
drunk.

Yolanda and Melissa came up for
air. She was drunk.

"Good morning, Yolanda."

"Nova! When did you get here?
How long have we been here,
Melissa?"

Melissa ran her hands through
Yolanda's short, graying hair.

"I have something to show you, but I can't pull it out," said Nova. "You'll just have to look under my cloak real fast. You'll never believe what I've got under my cloak. Promise not to tell anyone."

"Melissa, have you met my good friend, Nova?"

"He introduced us, Yolanda. Remember? It is always a pleasure to meet you, Nova. My name is still Melissa. I am still going to be an artist. No one has hired me, yet, not even a poor family looking for a death mask for an infant."

She leaned into Yolanda's shoulder with drooping eyelids. Melissa pressed her lips into the older woman's neck.

"Yolanda, listen. Look under my cloak," said Nova. "You won't believe what you see."

"I never like to hear that," said Yolanda. "It never ends well."

"Do it!"

She pulled the cloak back and looked. He angled his body so she could see the object jammed into his belt, sleeping against the frayed cloth of his dirty clothes like a mantis.

"It's an axe."

"Not so loud! You want me to be arrested? You'll never believe who gave it to me!"

"Why are you carrying an axe?"

"Not so loud! Look, I won't be carrying it tomorrow. I'll give it back once the body starts to stink. Then, I won't need it. It won't take long in this damp weather. One more night, maybe one more after, and then the stink will pour through the walls, and no one will want the body after that."

Yolanda took a long drink of wine. She finished the wine. She held the empty cup out to Nova. "You're buying me a drink or else I'll shout about the axe."

"Not so loud! I already bought you a drink! Pietro gave me the axe."

"He was here. He was here, earlier. He tried to lead us in song."

"He gave it to me as casually as I'm scratching my ear."

"Viri! More wine! Real wine!"

Melissa smiled like a minx. "I've heard everything, you know. You're going to have to buy my silence, too. How come someone died and none of us heard about it? No one is missing. Who composed the eulogy? Who painted the death mask?"

"Suicide. A beautiful young woman, too, so an undertaker's wife would have handled the corpse."

Yolanda smacked Nova's arm. "I have an idea! Melissa, I have an idea! I have a wonderful idea, worthy of Caligari himself!"

Poets drowned the tavern out with their jeers and boos. Someone had composed a eulogy to a young woman's breasts.

An undertaker woke up in the corner. He staggered to his feet, and limped to the cluster of poets. The undertaker punched the first poet he saw. The poet fell back onto the ground. The jeering silenced. The undertaker vomited violently into the nearest spittoon. He wiped his face with his sleeve. The undertaker grimaced. He stepped to the bar.

The huge man leaned against the bar next to Melissa. He bought a drink to rinse his mouth out with it into the spittoon.

Viri had a bill ready for the undertaker. The undertaker had a huge bill. He pulled a heavy purse from his pocket, and tossed plenty of coins on the counter.

The poet he had punched, smacked him on the back. "Where did you

get so much coin, when no one else
has died for days?"

"Someone died."

"What?" said the poet. "Who did
they hire for the eulogy? Who
painted the death mask?"

The undertaker had a grim reply.
"My wife was the only one got any
work out of her. She sent me here
to stay out of her way."

"Those foolish women toying with
melancholy..." The poet grabbed
the undertaker's collar as if it was
the undertaker's fault. "What do
they think they are, poets? Suicide
is our fate, and ours alone.
Caligari would have broken into
the catacombs and beaten her
corpse to a pulp were he still
alive."

"Caligari was a ghoul, and a hack.
Artists and undertakers don't
pretend to feel love for the dead."
The hungover man was three
times the size of the poet, and he

had no difficulty brushing aside
the poet's hand.

Melissa touched the undertaker's
leg. "I'm going to be an artist, you
know."

The old man snorted at her. "Buy
your own drinks. I'm married to a
good woman."

"Exactly my point! You need to buy
drinks for a no-good woman!"

He laughed. He tossed a single
coin onto the counter for her.

Melissa clapped for the
undertaker. She kissed his cheek.
She lifted the glass to her
benefactor and toasted him.

He shoved his way past the poets,
past the artists, and into the
morning street, where the people
who do not deal in death gave the
man a wide path.

The lime and rot smell of death
and catacombs hung over all the
undertakers, all the poets, and all
the artists. It hung over Nova, too,

and all the orphans stranded in
the tombs.

Yolanda leaned into Melissa.

"I love artists best of all," said
Melissa. "Can I borrow some paint
crystals and papyrus? Then, you
can hold very still and I will
pretend that you are dead – which
will make me very sad – but it will
give me a chance to practice my
trance. Then, I can show patrons
my work, and they will hire me to
paint death masks. Then, I can
buy you drinks in penitence for
stealing all your clients."

Viri touched Melissa's arm. "You
don't have to practice on the living
today. One of the poets is turning
thirty tomorrow. He plans to go
out in full Caligari style: top hats
and tails, absinthe, and dancing
until he hangs himself from a tree.
You can paint him hanging from
the breeze, and try to capture his
death on a flat canvas. Maybe even
cut him down, do a proper death
mask."

Yolanda touched Nova's arm. "Will you come, or will you go to sleep again?"

"Sleep," said Nova. "I have to work again at dog hour."

Yolanda smacked Nova's arm. "Wait! I remember! I had an idea as horrible as your axe!"

"Not so loud, Yolanda!"

"I want you to let Melissa paint the death mask of the suicide girl. She went into your tomb, right? You can sneak us in and I'll teach her to paint the soul by candlelight. And it will be so beautiful. I'll teach her how to heat the crystals and move the brush fat over thin and her tormented soul will get a proper memorial."

"No."

"Please?"

"I can't."

"I'll tell about your axe."

"Yolanda, don't ask me that," said Nova. "I can't."

"Think about it. We'll come visit you tonight. We promise we won't steal anything."

"You know I can't let you into the tomb."

"Melissa needs the practice. Even suicides deserve a death mask. People should remember the people they love, even if they did something horrible."

"Spoken like a true artist, who profits from memorials."

Melissa grabbed Yolanda by the nose. "He says he can't. Maybe he already sold the corpse to a wizard in the night. You aren't paying close enough attention to me, Yolanda. I may fall in love with someone else."

"You need to paint more or you'll never make it as an artist."

"We're drunk. If you don't help me,
I'll be sober!"

"We need to go to the suicide party
right now, before we start to sober.
Is the sun up? Viri! Why haven't
we all gone to the suicide party?"

"Ask them! They're hanging
around here and they're not even
buying anything anymore. They're
just yelling at each other and
throwing my stuff around."

"Nova, go ask them when the
suicide party starts. We don't want
to miss the party."

"I'm going home."

"We'll see you after the party.
Promise me you'll help Melissa.
Let her in to practice the death
mask. We won't steal anything. We
won't defile the dead. We're not
witches. We're artists who provide
a vital service to the families of the
deceased. She needs the practice."

"Don't push him," said Melissa.
"He's not a poet. He's not an artist.

He's more like an undertaker than us. He's respectable."

Nova Coates snorted at them. "Have fun at your suicide party. I hate those things. Undertakers don't go to them, do they?"

"Never."

"I am like an undertaker, then. Undertakers and tomb guards care for the body. Artists and poets care for the soul. Also, undertakers and tomb guards get paid steady, while you are waiting for another war or plague or catastrophe like vultures to devour wealthy patrons who can afford the luxury of a death mask and eulogy."

"Best to Marducci," said Yolanda. "Haven't seen him in a while. Thanks for the wine."

Nova stood up carefully so his axe wouldn't clatter on any of the furniture. He liked carrying an axe. It reminded him of the war, when his whole life was ahead of

him like a thundercloud, and
arrows blotted out the sun, and
adrenaline filled his body with a
fire he had never since known and
in between the fighting, the long
nights in tents chasing bliss
against death. Marducci, always
Marducci.

Nova touched the axe, and
remembered Marducci dancing
like a gypsy at a soldier's campfire
in a stolen dress and everyone
laughing.

Nova walked home alone.

Nova rented his little room among
many rooms. Children ran like
thieves through the halls,
squealing at each other. Women
chased them with spoons and
belts, laughing with them. Nova
slid into darkness, where he kept
his window shuttered tight, and he
imagined the silence of the
catacombs, where he stayed
awake. In these loud halls, he slept
until darkness came.

Nova looked up at the death mask
of his father on the wall after he

woke up. Yolanda had painted it
on the second day. Father, as Nova
really knew him: an old, tired man
with sad eyes and a sardonic twist
to his mouth. Ruddy papyrus skin,
all sun-bruised and leathery, held
into layer after luminous layer of
jeweled paint. Blue veins ran along
the temples. Old welts and scars
swelled under the surface of the
skin. Yolanda had called him a
wounded soul, with so many dead
loves and only one son surviving
the war, who would leave no heir
behind. The memory of Nova's
brothers was a distant pain. He
regretted the war when he thought
of them, even as he loved the war
for the exhilaration of it and
meeting Marducci.

The death mask's eyes glowed like
haunted things, even in the
darkest night masks were
beautiful, like poetry you could
drink with a gaze. Yolanda had
painted the mask and charged
almost nothing. She was flush with
coin from the end of the war and so
many sons returning wounded,

dying, and dead. She was
fascinated by the old man's ruined
face, with so much grief.

Nova pulled a bottle of brandy
from under his bed. It was almost
empty. He drank what was left. He
ate stale bread and bruised apples.
He drank another bottle of wine.
Then he drank some laudanum. It
helped him sleep. He drank most
of the bottle of laudanum. His
hand lingered on the axe, even as
he slept.

Somewhere in the city, poets wrote
eulogies for their suicidal friend,
and musicians and actresses
danced with artists and actors and
the bushes trembled with wanton
embraces and the absinthe flowed
like a green waterfall.

Caligari's ghost was seen on four
separate occasions, pinching young
men's buttocks, and leaping into
the shadows in top hat and long-
tailed jacket and nothing else. The
harmonium and the guitar and the
xylophone and the snickering
snare drum rolled to improvised
climaxes like an orgy in the

evening twilight.

Finally, the suicidal poet pulled his scroll from his cape. He climbed the ladder, with trembling hands and tears streaming down his face. The music stopped. The poet took off his hat so his friends could place the rope around his neck. He put the hat back on, and tied small bits of string to his ears so the fine top hat would stay on his head when he kicked his own ladder away to die. First, before death, he had to recite his eulogy. "I dance with ghosts when I dance alone! I'll dance until my legs are stones..."

There was weeping. There was music and weeping. There was dancing and weeping. There was poetry and weeping.

Then, the poet shouted out two final words: "For Caligari!"

The party shouted it in refrain over and over. "For Caligari! For Caligari! For Caligari! For..."

The poet kicked his ladder away.
He held the scroll in his hand, so it
could fall from his fingers like in a
dramatic poem, tumbling into the
cool, night breeze.

4

Nova was asleep long before
sunset, and before the poet's death.
When the crier woke him up, he
wrapped the cloak around his
shoulders. He picked up his ash
staff. He checked his lamps for
lilac oil, and re-filled the one
burned down last night. He walked
through the empty streets of dog
hour, to the main gate.

On the hill above the catacombs,
the poet's body still hung from the
tree, with cap and fine suit and
sheaves of paper all around the
dangling feet, of all the eulogies
written by the poets for their
friend and all of them damp from
tears and from the light rain that
had been a harbinger of storms to
come.
The clouds smothered the full

moon. The air was pregnant with rain that refused to fall. The wind was strong.

Nova picked his way through the sleeping bodies on the hill high above the catacombs. He kicked a harmonium aside, and peeled Yolanda from the body of an actress. She choked a little, and snored. Green vomit clung to her lips like a fungus. Nova dragged her away from the heap and rolled her onto her side so she wouldn't choke in her own vomit. He stole someone's cloak and covered her with it, to keep her warm. He went back, searching for Melissa.

Nova found her at the edge of the party. She had bent over a prone man. A candle burned beside her.

"Melissa?"

"Nova? You missed the party. I skipped the absinthe. I haven't had a drop since daybreak."

"Was it a good party?"

"It was a wonderful party.
Everyone was crying because it
was so wonderful. This man was
the poet's lover. He cut his wrists.
He was a drummer. He had such
strong hands. He drove a knife into
his own wrist in mourning and
bled his life away. Look at his face.
Look how beautiful he is in such
agony."

Nova brought his lamp closer. He
saw that she had spread papyrus
over the dead face already. She
was warming the paint in her
palm. The color crystals melted
like cheap chocolates in her body
heat.

"You have to go to work, don't
you?"

"I do."

"Did you come here to find Yolanda
and me before you left?"

"I did."

"Yolanda said you had an axe."

"I do."

"Can you cut down the poet for me? I know it isn't polite, but no one will mind when they see why. I want to paint his death mask, too, before the crows ruin his beautiful face."

Melissa touched a paint crystal with the tip of her finger. She licked the paint off. She plucked a brush from her cloak and began to work on the papyrus with the paint, to capture the skin tones and subtleties of the soul beneath the skin.

"Do you know how I met Yolanda? When, my father died. Yolanda painted his mask, and befriended me. Yolanda showed me where the tavern was, and I had a place I could make more friends. I didn't know I could go anywhere smelling like death until she showed me."

"Did you?"

"You're not really listening,

Melissa. I can tell you anything. I can tell you that you're beautiful. I can tell you that Yolanda is beautiful. I can tell you that all of you are so beautiful. I wish I could live like you do, in beauty, for beauty."

"Beautiful…"

"Yolanda painted my father's death mask. She helped me find the best poet I could afford for the eulogy. She helped me carry him into the catacombs. Afterwards, she showed me Viri's tavern, and I started drinking there. I made friends. I found you there, and remembered you from the catacombs, when you stole bread from me, when you had no place to live and you were still an orphan. I met you again at the tavern, and introduced you to Yolanda."

"I love Viri's."

"I'll cut the poet down for you. Can you bring me their masks, when you come to me in the catacombs? Can you bring me the masks, and leave Yolanda here. I'll let you

paint the dead girl's mask, too,
before it really starts to rot."

She was listening now. Her brush
hand stopped. "You will?"

"I will."

"Some artists go their whole lives
and never paint more than
merchants and stevedores, and I
will paint the niece of a Doge."

Melissa looked up from her work.

"I'll bring you the masks, Nova. I'll
make sure they're beautiful. Go cut
down the poet before the crows
find him. Get to your tomb. I'll find
you there, before daybreak."

Nova left her there, hunched over
the dead musician, chasing the
death mask artist's trance.

Nova placed his lamp on the
ground below the poet's tree, and
rested his ash staff beside it. He
pulled the axe from his belt,
unafraid of who might be watching

among the fallen drunks. He lifted
the ladder out from under the pile
of damp eulogies. He climbed up
beside the dangling corpse, to chop
at the rope at the branch. The axe
was sharp and the rope was cheap.
In two swift strikes, the dead poet
collapsed in his heap of paper. His
top hat bent against the ground.
His cape smothered his pained face
and bruised neck. If someone
didn't know better, they'd think he
was just another dreamer, in an
absinthe fog below the tree.

Nova put the axe back under his
cloak, and picked up the lamp, the
staff.

Around the tree, all the people
were dreaming in a green haze,
sleeping like beautiful monsters in
the grass. All of them danced and
fornicated and chased oblivion
until oblivion caught up with them
in a spider web of sleep.

Nova remembered battlefields.
Nova remembered his father
sleeping in death, white lips from
the diphtheria and a thousand
pounds thinner.

Nova remembered the orphans
sleeping in the middle of the dark
hallways, like Melissa had slept,
among the rats and the dead. Nova
remembered when the men slept
before a battle - all of these men
fallen with their eyes closed like
they were practicing death, like
how soldiers drilled for everything
a thousand times before anything
happened.

Caligari's naked shade flittered
away in the night like a black cat
chasing a black bird through the
dark places in the underbrush.

Nova picked up a bottle of absinthe
from a sleeping man's palm. He
drank the single finger that was
left inside, night cool and watered-
down with the saliva of a dozen
dreamers. He threw the empty
bottle towards the moon. It
shattered somewhere, far away.

To work, then, until Melissa came.

5

Pietro looked worried. Nova was a little late, but that wasn't what had Pietro worried. The old man clutched at his ash staff, and he had lit his second lamp to increase the light in the narrow hall. He sat between the lamps. "About time you showed up, Nova. I was worried a wizard might have snatched you up. You still have the axe?"

Nova pulled his cloak to the side and turned. The axe dangled from his belt like a tail.

"Good. Good. Anything comes near you, you pull that axe out right away. And make sure your staff is close at hand. Ash staff and lilac fire, like in the holy books. We don't want any wizards finding us here, coming after the body. Axe'll scare off his cronies. Make sure you keep that door closed."

"You all right, Pietro?"

"I'm fine. I'm fine. Shift's over. I'm fine. Heard lots of noise, though.

Catacombs are supposed to be quiet, Nova. Keep yourself safe."

"Do you want your axe back?"

"Not tonight, Nova. No rot stink, yet. You keep it and be ready. We've got to keep that door closed. Got to keep it closed, and keep the lilac-fire burning long and long."

"Good night, Pietro."

"Good night, Nova."

Pietro's whistling filled the catacombs, and echoed through the halls. Nova realized Pietro whistled to make sure he never surprised anyone in the dark. They'd all hear him coming - have time to hide. Nova had heard stories about wizards when they were interrupted.

Nova had heard terrible stories about wizards. Everyone had. Monstrous men, consumed by the demons they had bargained with for power, dark arts with terrible

red eyes. They seemed smaller
because they scared Pietro.
Anything that scared Pietro was
nothing, at all. Hedge wizards sold
charms along the roads, and they
all seemed fake to Nova. None of it
seemed to be anything but
religious muttering. Still, there
were such things, and Nova's job
was to protect the noble tombs
from necromancy as much as it
was to protect it from grave
robbers.

Nova watched the lamp. Nova
couldn't sit down comfortably with
the axe jammed in his belt. He
held it in one hand, and watched
the lilac light fill the hall with a
gentle sweetness that only made
the sick smell everywhere harder
to bear. The damp rot crept
through Nova's hair, and his
beard, and his cloak and tunic. In
a drunk sweat, the catacombs
poured out from his body, worse
than an undertaker's lime and
myrrh.

Nova waited for Melissa to come to
him, in the tomb.

6

Melissa had lived in the catacombs
for years, after her family died in
the war. When Nova first worked
here, she tried to sell herself to
Nova for food. Nova refused her,
and gave her nothing. He tried to
chase her away with a growl. She
returned enough to him to learn
his name and steal from him and
tell him all about the men that
would buy someone so young.

In the tavern, Yolanda met
Melissa when Melissa was trying
to convince Nova to buy her a
drink. Instead, Yolanda did.
Melissa had been trying to fall in
with death mask artists, and had
been in the tavern to do exactly
that. Yolanda didn't seem to mind,
and the two had formed a genuine
connection that Nova could tell. It
was as genuine as any friendship,
at least, and Melissa could have
left Yolanda for another mentor
with her good looks if she wanted
to do so. She had stayed with
Yolanda a long time.

Nova waited for Melissa for what
seemed like most of his shift. She
had two masks to paint, first, and
that took long, careful brush
strokes for a beginner. She wasn't
as fast as Yolanda.

Yolanda was breathtaking at her
work. Nova had seen it.

Yolanda painted beautiful, lifelike
faces in barely an hour. She
captured ladybugs between swift,
deft fingers and she melted swirls
of paint upon their backs before
they could escape her thumb and
forefinger. Yolanda painted a
single petal of a morning-glory and
studied for days in wonder at how
the paint swirled around the living
petals while the sun warmed the
flower open and the stars cooled it
closed. Yolanda studied the
movement of the flower's soul
inside the luminescent paints.

Yolanda was a master, who
painted the death masks of Doges.
Yolanda would have likely painted
the suicide girl's death mask, if the
girl had fallen ill of cholera or

something slower and venereal,
like the other girls of her caste.

Yolanda always wept for the
beautiful girls. She spent days in
the fields, crying and smearing
paint over insects and flowers in
the spring, or falling leaves or
icicles in the colder seasons.
Yolanda took pity on her clients,
like she had when she took lonely
Nova to the tavern after the death
of his father. She helped carry the
dead to the tombs if there weren't
enough able-bodied bearers. She
helped them find priests and poets
and a reliable orphan to guide
them into the tombs.

After a long, unbroken silence,
footsteps echoed down the hall. A
lamplight flickered like ghosts
against the bricks. Melissa, in the
top hat and tails of the dead poet,
and one of Yolanda's better
dresses, but very muddy, strolled
down the catacomb alone. She
carried Yolanda's satchel on her
back, with the papyrus strips and
the paint crystals and the finishing

oils and the thickeners and thinners that she would mingle together like cake frosting into a death mask.

Nova stood up for her.

"I was worried you'd never make it in time," he said.

"I thought I'd change, to be respectful of her. I brought you the masks. They aren't very good, I'm afraid. I'll get better. I just need practice. Yolanda will keep helping me. She already has me painting the backs of cockroaches while they're running past. They're so fast, you wouldn't believe it, but Yolanda can paint a gorgeous swirl of soul before they can escape into the walls."

She slipped two masks out from under her coat. One had misshapen lips, and strange circles under its eyes, as if it were very tired. The other mask was purple, as if she had gotten her color crystals misaligned in her palm.

"In my defense, I was working by

candlelight in a field between
rainstorms. Keep them anyway.
You can sell them when I'm as
famous as Yolanda. You said you
would let me in?"

"Yes."

"She's going to be on the floor,
right? They don't wall off the
suicides. She'll be easy to find. I'll
have to fight some rats, but I'll
paint their teeth if they give me
trouble. I'll paint their eyes closed,
and they'll run away, blind."

"She should be right in the middle
of the floor, just as you walk in."

"When they return with the bodies
of her family, they'll crush her
corpse with their boots and grind
her into dust for what she did."

"How long will you need?"

"I'll work fast, I promise. And, if
shift ends here before I'm done, tap
on the door, and I'll just have to
find a place to curl up and sleep a

while. I haven't slept since yesterday. Here, take the masks and do what you want with them. They aren't very good, and they'll be worth nothing to you until I'm famous, like Yolanda."

Nova took a deep breath. He slipped the masks into the cloak pockets, beside his flasks. He looked around the hallway. He half expected Pietro to jump out at him like a maniac, screaming about the door and the wizards and the thieves. He took the key from his belt. He unlocked the door.

He saw no one. He opened the door slowly, and just enough to let Melissa inside. It seemed like any other door. It wasn't stiff or loud. It felt strange, doing it after keeping it closed for so long.

Melissa slipped through.

He closed the door quickly behind her.

Nova heard a wet thump.

He heard Melissa gasp in pain.

The door trembled from an impact of something large slamming against the door.

Nova clenched his axe. He pulled open the door, hard.

Melissa's body slid where it had fallen after bouncing off the ash door. Her eyes were frozen in a gasp of shock, and pain. Nova lifted his torch up. He gazed into the black, as surprised as his dead friend.

An animal growled from a shadow.

Two red eyes pierced the darkness beyond the lilac flame.

A wizard was inside the tomb. It curled away from the lilac light wrapped in darkness. The wizard's red eyes were like burning brimstone flames. Magic spilled out from its body like a cape of demonic tentacles. The cape curled away from the lilac flame, dripping black jelly that steamed in the lilac light.

Nova dropped the axe. He pulled
the lamp from the end of the staff.
He swung the staff towards the
monster in the dark,
threateningly. They were nowhere
near each other.

"Get back! Demon, get back!"

The wizard stepped back deeper
into the catacombs and curled his
lips into a toothy, menacing frown.
His voice was red silk. "Leave fool."
His stance, beneath his demonic
shroud was familiar. It was still
wearing the funeral garb from the
night before.

Nova recognized the wizard when
he frowned. This wizard picked up
the corpse of his own daughter, one
leg in each hand. The corpse was
vivisected into two halves, each
stiff as wood, with organs frozen
inside as if pressed against a glass.

A tentacle braved the lilac flame to
clutch Melissa's ankle. Nova was
too shocked to move against it. He
didn't know how to move against

it. He watched wisps of steam peel off from the tentacle where the lilac flame burned it. He watched the tentacle tug at Melissa's foot. Then, like a bird taking flight, the wizard whirled away into darkness, away from the lilac light and the ash staff and the door and Nova's place in the catacombs.

Melissa's smeared blood raced off into the catacombs like a wild stroke of paint.

Nova closed the door. He looked down at all the blood there. He lifted Melissa's death masks out of his cloak's pockets, up to his face in the lilac lamp light. He gazed at the deformity of them, and the amateurishness of them. People shouldn't remember Melissa like that, he thought.

Nova shattered the two death masks like plates. He stomped on them, until the tiny pieces were just bits of dust soaking in Melissa's blood.

Tears, then.

Nova lit the second lamp and placed it so he would have no part of himself in shadow. He sat in the center of the lilac flames. He clutched at his holy ash staff, with the holy ash door shut behind him. He whispered half-remembered prayers to a goddess he barely knew. He trembled, terrified. He wept for his dead friend. He wished he could compose a eulogy for her.

His surly replacement came, eventually. The fellow put his lamp down next to one of Nova's. He picked Pietro' axe off the ground, and slid it under his cloak like plucking a flower. It chinked against something metal. He moved carefully, though, to avoid the blood that crept from beneath the door. He had noticed the blood right away, and the two lamps burning.

"You let someone in there, didn't you?" he said.

Nova said nothing.

"I did once, too. It was a long time ago. You thought our job was to keep people out of the tomb."

Nova tried to speak, but he couldn't. Tears choked him silent.

"Know what we're really here to do? We keep it inside. We keep the ash door lit with lilac fire, and we keep everything inside. You won't be in trouble for letting someone in. I know. As long as you didn't let anyone out, you won't be in trouble."

"I saw the wizard. I saw him with my own eyes. I saw him. He spoke to me. I know who he is, too."

"Don't tell me anything else. I don't want to know. I'm glad I never saw him. When I heard what was happening inside, I figured it out. My brother was too tough to go down like he did unless it was a wizard. Nothing I could have done to save him. I kept the door closed. Poor bastard. Nothing you can do now. What's your name?"

"Nova Coates."

"My name is Caligari. Just Caligari."

"Like the poet?"

"Who?"

"The famous poet, Caligari?"

"Never heard of him. You'd best get out of here. Find a road, and keep walking."

"Yeah. I need to run to water. I need to wash the scent of my soul in the sea to keep it from knowing me. I've never even seen the ocean. I don't know where it is. Good night, Caligari."

"Bye, Nova. Nice knowing you. Wait, one more thing."

Nova turned, and this man he had seen every night for years, though they had never before exchanged a word produced a bag of coins from his cloak and tossed them through the air. Nova caught the coins, and felt their implausible weight. He had just been given a small fortune by a stranger. Nova took the coins silently.

Nova bowed to his new friend. Nova couldn't imagine how anyone could have so many coins in their pockets, and give them away so casually to a stranger.

Life was full of the impossible. Moments lined up in madness, and dissolved in madness. Walking, as if on the edge of a rope, whistling like Pietro, trying to act like everything was fine, he was terrified and walked faster and faster.

Outside, the suicide dreamers on the hill had only just begun to peel themselves away from their oblivions.

Yolanda was not awake, yet. She slept beneath the cloak, and already her head looked swollen from the migraine that she'd wear like a crown for the rest of the day. Her painting supplies were lost to the catacombs, now. She'd have to buy new tools. She'd wake up with a terrible migraine, look for her tools, and believe Melissa had stolen them. Yolanda would wake up betrayed by her beloved.

Nova hated that. He hid coins in her pockets to cover the lost supplies - more than enough.

Nova didn't go home. He walked back to the city limits, to the side gate. He gave his cloak to the first orphan he saw. He gave the empty lamp to the second. He walked to where Marducci was still on duty for a little while longer. Marducci nodded. Nova sat just outside the city, waiting on a patch of grass for his friend to finish his night. The two men silently nodded at each other.

When Marducci's replacement came, Nova walked off, away from the city. He didn't look over his shoulder. His lover – his oldest friend in the world – was ten paces behind him.

"We're out enough. What's wrong?"

"I'm leaving, Marducci. I'm leaving immediately. I won't even go home to gather my things."

"Why? What did you do?"

"I have to go, right now. You told me you would follow me once, through the sea of blood, to the gates of hell. You promised me that, in the war. Will you come with me, Marducci? I don't want to face this alone."

"What did you do?"

"I see. Can you do me one favor, very small and almost completely legal?"

"Anything."

"My father's death mask will get stolen. Someone will take it. Someone will sell it on the street, who didn't know my father."

"Go back to your room and get it," said Marducci. "I'll come with you."

"I can never return to the city. I should have left hours ago. But you can return. Please, take my father's death mask to Yolanda. Tell her that Melissa is dead, and there was nothing I could do to save her. Tell Yolanda that I'm so sorry. I'm so sorry about everything."

"Did you kill her?"

"What do you think?"

"Who's Yolanda?"

"She's a famous artist. Yolanda painted my father's death mask."

"I've never heard of her."

"She's the greatest artist in the city. Her death masks are jewels of paint. Ask around. Everyone knows her who works among the beautiful and the dead. I'm sorry, Marducci. Thank you for everything. I do love you. Good-bye."

"Nova...!"

Then, Nova was running. Nova was faster than Marducci. Once upon a time, Nova would have let Marducci catch him over and over, but not now. Nova ran with an adrenaline fear of death. Marducci fell behind, running in confusion from a world gone mad but unafraid. Marducci slowed when his lungs burned. Marducci leaned into a tree to catch his wind and watched.

Nova ran into a sunrise, past caravan tents, and farms, and out among the long roads and new places in the world, and all alone.

I WILL TRADE WITH YOU

The north star is still in my palm.

North, I keep on, but there's no
way to know how far I walked
before I stopped to rest on this
lump of sand instead of that one. I
need to rest to keep walking with
these old, uncertain bones. When
I'm ready to move again, I crawl a
little, and wait for my legs to work
right below me. When I can't walk
anymore, I drink my own blood
from my boots and joints like my
only water. I was not put together
well, nor will I ever be again.

Lady or the Tiger, Death Mask and Eulogy,

and Other Re-Imaginings

I do not know how many days
there were before this, but it has
only been a few days while I
walked, and then it was night, and
I slept sometimes during the night.
Then it was day again and I kept
on, where my hand still leads me.

My old right hand is still mine. It
was my first trade.

My legs are shorter than I
remember and it is hard to walk on
them when they are this worn
down. The sand slips through the
cracks of very old boots. I'm
bleeding somewhere in there, but
most of it stays in my boots and I
can drink it later. When I rest, I
can drink blood to keep going. It's
all I have to drink.

Let this body be numb and
unknown to me. There was little I
could do about it in the middle of a
desert. I licked what I could reach
of my blisters and sores and ill-
fashioned joints, drinking back my
own fluids. It hurt, but it had to be
done.

At night, the sand still held the
heat from the long afternoon. My
bare chest shivered in the frigid
desert wind. My feet cooked inside
of my boots. I walked and walked
licking the blood from my chin.

A wound from a sand lizard.

I had been traveling with the first
new northerners, I had met. Three
hard male faces and her beauty
walking down the street like it was
such a common thing for the
people of the north to walk

through damp, sweltering Tavis on a late summer day.

I couldn't tell the three men apart and I didn't know what to think about that. I thought she was beautiful, and I thought quite a lot about that. Maybe she was like them, but better at trading, or maybe she had never traded for anything in her life and that's how she was so beautiful. It's hard to tell with people of the north when you haven't been around them all your life.

At the time, I picked grapes during the day and slipped back into the vineyards after dark when no one was around. I sold the night grapes to other travelers before shuffling off, exhausted, to sleep at the edge of the fields until the overseer whipped me awake. I was

saving up for passage to the
mountains I had seen on a map
halfway across the world. I was
going north, halfway home, to the
mountains.

I had heard tales of cities carved
from ice and marble in the north
all the days of my life. I had only
ever known the salt marsh and
swamps and rocky hills above the
lakes, where I had grown up
almost completely alone but for my
mother and an old sailor.

I had high hopes when I saw the
four newcomers. I followed them to
a sailor's tavern, and found a place
to be with her alone after a while,
and I mentioned it to her in the
tavern, that I wanted to go north
to the mountains halfway home, as
soon as I can work up enough and
save.

"I know a few people that could help you over the mountains," she had said. Her eyes creased beyond my shoulder.

I turned and saw a dead rat, smashed into the floor. I hadn't noticed it before. She whispered a prayer to a god or goddess I did not know to aid the rat that I would have killed if I saw it first.

"You wish to escape this filthy place," she said. "We should all see Great Valion's Gates before we die. It's such a beautiful city, cut from white marble and ice by master carvers and there's so many winter roses growing in the ice. You can travel together with my friends," she said. "We're parting ways here."

I frowned at that. "What about you?"

"I've been there before," she said, as if that was some kind of answer to the question I was asking.

I felt the north star even indoors and drunk. I knew exactly where it was above my head. I knew where north was in a hand I had traded with an old sailor.

~~~

I had fallen asleep after drinking too much wine, probably drugged wine, in a forest near a campfire. I woke up in a desert, with nothing around me but sand as far as I could see and only my hand felt familiar to me.

A large lizard lounged on my chest like a lover. It had yellow eyes with the expressionless languor of a lizard. As good a friend as any I had met lately, I thought. We stared at each other with faces unreadable to each other.

Then, for the reasons known only to lizards, it had been waiting for me to look at it before its feast began. It did not wish to eat me unless I was still alive. It finally opened its mouth. The long tongue stretched over my face, licking at the salt of my boils and blisters. The gnarled head turned sideways, and it chose the nearest flesh it had. The lizard took slow bites of my chin.

I couldn't feel the pain, yet, or

move away.

I saw the bloody teeth. The lizard's
casual prongs upon my flesh were
of a lazy, summer lunch, just
before a siesta. The forks came
down and poked the sides of beef.
The diner was alone on his
sunswept balcony, and ate with a
methodical quiet of purpose. The
meat didn't feel, and didn't scream,
but the meat wanted to very much
jump and scream and fight back.

I had drunk too much and it had
probably been drugged. My body
was numb and had taken so long
to wake up for me because much of
it was new to me. My right hand
was not new. The chewing was a
distant pain, like feeling
something noxious on the breeze.
It should hurt more. Everything
should hurt more. It would when
the body woke up to itself in full.

I regained my hands slowly. I
lifted the numb clubs with sleepy
fingers and I pushed at the beast
upon my chest. Then, my fingers
could hold on a little. Then they
could hold on very strong. I could
sit up slowly with this slowly
wriggling beast in my powerful
arms.

I choked the lizard.

My little friend wiggled and kicked
and scratched at me but not for
very long. I watched the golden
light in his eyes fade to numb.

I poked at my shredded chin and
thought about bandaging myself
with a shirt. I picked up the
lizard's cadaver instead.

At the very least I had something
to eat out here, and something else
to think about while I walked and
drank. Blood would be my only
water for a long time in these long,
hot dunes.

I took my shirt off. I had good
leather worker's clothes once, that
fit me like a glove after so long in
the vinyards, but now all I had
was a white shirt and burlap
leggings. I wrapped the shirt over
my skull to keep the worst of the
sun from striking my head. I
couldn't remember if I had hair as
I was traveling with the three men
or not. I don't think I did. I didn't
have it now.

I held the corpse of the lizard by
the tail. I slung it across my back
like a small sack, and ate it slowly
over a long day from the face to the

skull. The bones were inedible and I left them behind me for the sand to devour.

I walked.

When the sun fell to my left, I sat down and prayed to the gods of the north I did not know.

Nothing happened. The moon rose was all. Maybe that was a miracle tonight.

I looked up at the white crescent like a goddess' eye closing to me.

The hot sand still burned through my boots when I walked at night. At least the night air cooled my body down. I had never been to a desert before. I had heard stories. I didn't know which desert was beneath my feet, but there were many made new after the god had pushed the continents together.

My back wearied of the dead weight of my food so I ate much of my lizard raw, even though I did not hunger for it. Whosever stomach this was, it kept the rancid flesh down. I'd rather eat the meat raw than cook it. I didn't want to lose any liquid that could be considered wet enough to drink. The wetter an organ was, the better it was, no matter how awful it tasted.

I walked all night, always north.

When the peeking light of the sun appeared on the far side of the

sand dunes, I sat down. My skin
had bubbled like cooked meat,
then fallen into strips of frayed,
thin, dry leather. I was covered
with a thick layer of sweat-
congealed sand. At least the sand
helped keep the skin from bleeding
more.

On my back, I tried to cover as
much of my body as I could against
the sunlight with the shirt, but it
wasn't long enough to protect both
my head and my body. I tried
rolling in sand to get it to clump on
me. I closed my eyes. I dreamed of
Tavis, and the sound of the ocean
water crashing into the mighty
cutter ships that docked there,
looking for grapes and wine.

I had grown up near a salt lake
beach south of Tavis, where the
marsh is thick and every building

collapses into the marsh. The
sailors that came told half-witted
stories about cursed ships, never
allowed to return to land. They
talked about their glorious journey
to Galesberg before the shift like a
myth. They talked of the great god
of the continents, who had pulled
the lands together on a whim -
perhaps, to impress a mortal
woman, or to answer a pious
prayer of a sick child who wished
to visit Galesberg. The story
varied, but this was universally
known: The continents came
together one day in a terrible
earthquake everywhere in the
world, and everyone says the god
that did it was running over the
land, smiling and pushing the
rocks together like a luminescent
giant.

My eyes bulged wide at their tales
of storms and monstrous currents,
and horrific serpents that had once
scraped the sides of the salt-eaten

cutter ships when the shift came
and everyone and everything had
to adjust. People died that day in
the thousands, and in the days
afterward. But, the god had done
no more re-arranging after that,
and we all had to do our best to
move on. The maps were re-drawn.
The people all prayed for things to
hold still a little while more this
time.

And I lived on this long beach at
Tavis in the quiet afternoons after
studying in the temple all
morning. I sat with the old sailor.
He wore the same sun-drenched
red vest and woolen pants every
day of his life. He stank of coarse
sea salt from the lake where he
fished during the day with spears
and nets, wading out into fishkills
and trapweirs.

And there I learned the north star.

He pointed up at the sunlit sky
through an all-day drunk. "See
that up there," he said, "Do you see
that?"

I looked up where he pointed. I
saw only blue. "What?" I said.

"When the sun sets, that's where
the north star comes out." He
dropped his hand on me like an
anchor dropping. His voice rose
with the repetition of his myth of
youth. "We went all the way to
Galesberg because I could find that
damned little candle-point even on
the sunniest, cloudiest, ugliest,
prettiest day and night. I sleep,
and my hand just points." He lifted
his hand and shoved it into my
face. "It just points!"

I said nothing to him.

He stared at his hand a moment.
He took a drink.

He lifted his hand again, towards
me. "You can take my hand with
you!" he said, "Then you can sail
the sea anywhere and find that
stinking star."

"Will you tell me a story about the
lost sailor, and give me some of
your wine?" I replied, in my
sweetest boy voice.

"Take my hand," he shouted, "I'll
trade you yours for it!"

He took out a sharpened white

whale-bone.

"I like my hand," I said, "Yours is too old. Mother says I'm too young."

He shook his head at me and swayed back and forth. "But my hand has experience. You'll still live forever. We both will, if we are wise traders, and get better than we lose," he said, "but think of this: You'll always be able to find the north star. And I will get a hand that I can finally teach something new. I want to do new things. I don't want to think about Valion anymore." He lifted his blade. "If you're mother yells we can trade back. It's a crime you don't know what it feels like to have a homeland."

"Mother will yell," I said. "Tell me

about Valion, and maybe I'll feel it anyway."

"Valion is a jewel in a blighted world, but you'll never know!"

We did trade one day, after mother walked on beyond her own, tired skin. I stayed with him a while afterwards, and we traded then. It was my first trade, with the only other northerner I had ever known. He never wanted more than that.

~~~

I woke up in the desert again.

Full sun.

I tried to pray. I couldn't. My head
was swollen in the daylight heat,
and cluttered up the ancient
words. My tongue felt like a dry
mushroom in my mouth, and
refused to speak at all. My chin
gnawed on my exposed nerves like
the lizard's angry ghost. I squinted
my eyes. My deep red skin cracked
and screamed at me. White
continents of peeling skin cracked
and fell off my body and became
sand.

Did I fall asleep again? I don't
know. If I did, I dreamed in pink.
My eyelids draped over my eyes,
and I saw only the color of my skin
in the sun. I saw only pink. I
thought of nothing. I dreamed of
nothing. I felt everything.

When I didn't see any more pink, I
saw black. I opened my eyes, and

my hand pointed at the sky. I
dragged my tired bones together
and discovered my feet again,
beneath me.

Only sand.

I sat back down.

I drew letters in the sand with my
pointing hand, the one I had only
traded once. I wrote these lines out
for you to read, whoever listens.
The wind comes and blows the
little valleys of my words into a
smooth dune surface again. I write
and I pray. I pray and I write. And
the sand peels away my skin, my
voice, my words.

What else to tell you before my

sinews crackle and snap with
thirst, oh quiet Gods?

My hand writes. It writes well.
Here it is before you: my
miraculous message from the
sands.

I do not need the north star. I need
a different miracle from my hands.
I need help. Please, hands, bring
me water. Please, grant me the gift
of water. Let a rainstorm come. I
will lie down and open my mouth
and let the cool drops pour over my
naked body.

I will write the words.

Water. Water. Water.

Hills and valleys full of lazy

streams and fat rivers.

Yet, I have the voice of wind, and
no merciful God or Goddess hears
this sand and wind.

In Tavis, the gorgeous woman
whispered to her Goddess more
than she ever spoke to me. She
whispered with the throaty
rapture of the pigeons, and she
was praying for nothings. She
prayed for the soul of a dead rat,
mashed into the corner of a tavern.
She touched a beggar and prayed
for rain to clean his face. She
prayed for a good hair day in her
morning hand-mirror. I listened,
and lounged in her bed. I had
never known a woman from the
north countries before, and
wondered if it was supposed to be
different or better or worse than
the port women of the south. I

wanted to know. She seemed
willing to show me.

A firestorm rolled in from the
marsh, harmless and hot. Tongues
of tiny flames threaded out from
the sky, fizzling like baby sparks
where they fell into the damp
ground. She prayed that no sparks
would land on a dry rot plank and
burn a house down, but they rarely
did that. They came with the
rainstorms, in the summer.

"The gods ignore us in a firestorm.
It is a devil's reply to prayers," I
said, because I was looking for
anything to say at all.

"The gods always listen," she
replied, "I don't know. I keep
praying. We should always pray
because the spiritual lack inside of
us defines us no matter what we

wear. Pray because the emptiness
is what remains when everything
else can be made new."

I touched her hand, and prayed for
her love. I was listening to her
speak about her religion because I
was looking for an opportunity to
close the space between our faces.

Red firelight drifted all around her
pale skin. It died upon our bodies
like tiny chigger bites.

We pressed close in evening
twilight. The bees buzzed through
the fields of thickened grapes after
the firestorm passed. They drifted
through the open window of our
room, and landed upon our naked
skin. We watched, allowing them
to soak up the sweetness from her
body, for they meant no harm to

us.

She stared off behind me
somewhere. I had my eyes half-
closed so I could live in the bottled-
flower smell of her long neck. I
heard her soft whispers, and I
knew they weren't for me.

"What are you praying for?" I said.

"The bees," she said, "The poor,
ignorant bees that lick my
perfume."

"I think the bees are smarter than
we are," I said.

"I know they're not. Look at them,"
she said, "when you come here
tomorrow morning to pick the
grapes, they will sting at your

hand." She tapped my shoulder and pulled back from me. "And you! You will strike at the bees because you are ignorant, too."

"I am?" I said.

"Your hands pick the grapes," she said, "and the bees do not see that without men to pick grapes, there would be no vines at all."

"The bees are the worst part of it," I said, "them and the sun. I hate the sun." I look past her golden hair to the grapes in the twilight. "I wish we could work at night, but the overseer thinks we steal his grapes."

"You have admitted to me that you

do steal grapes. Without the bees, there would be no grapes," she said, "so you strike your own livelihood."

"There are always more bees," I said, "but there aren't always enough hands."

"Take mine," she said.

"What?" I pulled back from her. My hands drifted away from her white, linen dress like wind over drapes.

"I will trade with you," she said. She took my wrists, and lifted my hands up. "My hands won't strike the bees. I will take yours somewhere else. Then the poor bees will be safe at least from you."

"You have the hands of a woman,"
I said, "and if I took them, they'd
whither under the heat of the
workman's sun." I pulled my hands
away. I stepped back from her.
"These hands I have would swing
like pendulums at the end of your
arms. You would no longer be
beautiful."

"Then," she said, "just for a little
while?"

"No."

"Please?" She cocked her head and
her eyes sparkled in the angle of
the fading sun. "For the poor bees,"
she said, "and just for a while."

"People in this land do not trade hands," I said.

"It will just be for a little while," she said.

I felt the pull of my withered hand, to the north. Always north.

People in the southern country try to stay together for weeks, months, and years after spending a long evening in a tavern room. It was not the way of the northerners. It was not our way. She told me I should go or stay, but not to expect anything if I wouldn't trade with her.

"But you're so beautiful," I said.

"Beauty is for the young," she said.

"I've had enough of beauty."

Maybe she was the daughter of one of the three men. Maybe that is why they would not trade with her. My mother said that trade was never done between the flesh of a family, or those who know you when you're young. Trading is an act for equals.

In the morning the men had heard that I wanted to go to the old cities of the north, to Valion beyond the mountain of Petronus. I had to choose between her, indifferent to me and eating grapes that I had stolen at great personal risk, and these three hard men who could take me to the city I had heard about all the days of my life.

Three tall men whom she hugged

like brothers when we left her in
Tavis, and me whom she kissed on
the nose and told me I had a
beautiful nose and maybe when I
returned she would take it from
me.

Over a campfire, the men looked
exactly the same.

I asked them if they were brothers.

"No," said one of them, "we just
traded too much together. We all
look the same because we traded
too much."

"Do any of you have a name?" I
said.

Another one frowned. "I think I
used to be called Claret," he said,

"Somebody called me that once. After a while it's hard to remember. Mirrors don't work for us. Fortunetellers won't even talk to us to try and figure it out."

"No," said the first, "I was Claret. You tore my face off once and I turned into a monster and that woman from Valion called me Claret because I chewed off her first leg." He touched his nose, and pointed across the fire at his companion's face. "You and I traded noses and I got my face back and I felt human again. I'm Claret. You are someone else entirely."

"But who?" he said, "What are our real names now?"

"Who cares," said the third, "all I

know is I still have one hand left
that has always been mine. This
right hand is all mine."

"Can it find the north star?" I said.
I took another long drink from the
skein of wine.

"Sometimes, it can find anything,"
said the third. He took the wine
from me, and sipped. "Anything, I
want, it can find sometimes. Just
not always when I want it. It's
good to hold on to yourself as long
as you can."

We drank too much. I drank too
much. I listened. They talked. We
passed around the same skein of
wine. I drank and drank. They
sipped. Maybe they didn't drink
too much. They talked of trading
their souls for new souls like it was
as easy as trading cloaks. There

was a theological debate in Valion.
They had disagreed with the
woman. This is why they
separated.

Our eyes swirled with the same
secrets from the same skein. But I
drank too long each time. I took
more than my share. I was not an
even trader. I got greedy. I talked
to learn the limits of things, and
didn't know what I had never been
taught by my mother and the other
northerner in Tavis. I fell asleep,
and when I woke up with a lizard
on my chest under a desert sun.

~~~

I have two hands, and only one is
familiar to me. They write two
stories in the sand. That was my
left hand. My right hand took a

break to show me the north star. I looked up while I wrote with my left. They left the old right hand. Maybe this is the true piece of my old self, because it pulls me north.

My right hand returns to the dirt and writes.

I wonder what else they took from me. I should sit with them at their fire again, if I meet them. "My name is Lanval," I should say, "I still remember my name when my mother gave it to me. Now tell me what pieces of me you have taken that are mine. I do not begrudge them to you, for I was not a good traveling companion, but I would still like to know." Instead of killing them while they sleep, I will write my name on all the things they took in magic ink that never fades. Then, I will let them live, with my name wherever they

look and that will be worse than
death, because they will all lose
what is left of their old selves.

My right hand writes in the dirt,
and I have no hand-mirror to look
upon the face that looks back that
is not mine. I cannot pray, either,
except for this.

The woman of the north country.
She loved my eyes. She told me
that she loved my eyes. She sat on
my chest with her blonde hair
around us like a waterfall of light.
Her face was like a perfect white
moon in the center of her blonde
corona.

She told me I had gold-flecked blue
eyes like solar eclipses. She kissed
my eyebrows.

I pulled back from her kisses. "Where are you from, exactly? What city?"

"I am from Valion." She tried to kiss my eyebrows again.

"I didn't know that," I said. "I just thought you had visited it, once."

"You are from Valion, too," she said, "and that's another thing I like about your face." She kissed me on my nose.

"No, I'm from Tavis," I said, "Tavis born and raised. My mother might have been from Valion, or maybe my father, whoever he was." My eyebrows creased. I pulled away from her kisses again. "And what does that have to do with my face?"

"Lanval is the name of an ugly
bird, who sings all the songs of all
the birds with a beautiful voice,"
she said. "It is a good name for one
of us in a country that is not ours.
You are from Valion and you are
lying to me."

"Do you think I'm ugly? Do you
think I'm an ugly bird?"

She winked. "I am either from
Valion or Cape Brink, out upon the
ice. It is my hair that gives me
away, and your eyes that reveal
your homeland to me in Valion.
You would know these things if
you had been raised among us."

"Lies," I said, "All of them lies."

"All right," she said, "Where do you think I am from? Where do you think you are from? Do you think we just wandered out of the ground like this?"

"I think you are in fact an old man, who traded his body with some pretty young girls piece by piece. And I think you are from the beautiful girls of the whole world, all the prettiest ones."

"No," she said. "I really am from Valion."

"Do you ever think of going back there? Do you think my mother's family might really be from there or Cape Brink?"

She smiled. "You have beautiful eyes, like solar eclipses: a black iris in a dark blue sky. These are Valion eyes. They are more valuable than diamonds. Do not trade them for anything." She leaned down and kissed me on the bridge of my nose.

"You can have them," I said.

"I don't want your eyes," she said, "I could never see them like this if they were mine. You cannot see your own eyes."

"You could in a mirror."

"Then I would only remember you in them, and that is not the way of

our people. We do not know the
eyes of our fathers, if we even have
them."

I touched her body, all of it, and
felt the places where it could fall
apart with a sharp knife and come
together again. I had known
women, but I hated that she had
known men. I hated that I was not
the first one to discover this
amazing miracle that was her
curved lines, her beautiful hair
and flower perfume skin.

~~~

The three men walked with
uneven steps. Their footprints in
the dirt had different boot sizes. I
followed behind them with my
pack mule and felt uncomfortable
on the roads. They walked with
their covered wagons. I wanted to

get a horse before we left town, but they shook their heads.

"We can't ride in a saddle," said one of the men, "because our legs aren't really even, and nobody has the right saddle for us."

"Why aren't your legs even?" I said.

"Some legs wear down faster than others," said another one. "You'll see."

~~~

My eyes falter. Maybe they are not my own. They feel too old to be mine. My tears are not my own.

They come from these old eyes.

~~~

I left her in Tavis to find my
people's ancient city. I could have
stayed and drowsed against her
perfect skin. My right hand points
up at the north star while I sleep. I
try to hold it down. It shoots up
while I work, too. The small,
hooked blade in my hand to cut the
grapes from the vine points into
the burning sky in broad daylight
and I know that were the tip hangs
is the place the star waits behind
the blue curtain of daylight.

When I stole grapes at night, I had
to stand out under the stars first,
and let my right hand do it. That
way, when I was sneaking through
the vineyard, I could start at the
southern tip and always know my

way through to the north edge of the vineyards where I could sneak into the trees.

I felt the north star, all the time.

And the new mountains sat far north of Tavis. Galesberg was north-east, and Valion the beautiful white city of my people was beyond. And there I was, sleeping outside near a vineyard until the overseer whipped me awake for another day of work, looking up at the distant point of light tugging an invisible gossamer thread in my right hand. It lifted me up. I could feel it.

I should never have traded hands with that old drunk.

~~~

The other three men looked at where I aimed my weary, crooked finger.

"I used to sing songs about mermaids for an old man that had also come from the north," I said, "He talked of his life like a glorious myth. And it wasn't much, really. He got on a boat. The boat traveled to Galesberg before the continents came together. It was so glorious for him until the continents were moved. With one wave of a nostril hair, a god brought the continents together and all that glory was squat."

"I think you've had enough," said the third man, "because you have started to talk about religion with people you do not know well enough to talk to about religion. It is not our way. It is her way, not ours."

I took one more long drink. "I can't believe I left her," I said, "Do you want my hand so I can go home to Tavis?"

"Which one?" said the third man.

"My right one," I said.

"I already have a hand," he said, "and it is all I have left of my old self."

"Me, too," I said.

"You've had enough wine," he said, "because you are talking about gods and love and torturing yourself over it. She didn't try to stop you. Don't forget that. You are going to your home country. You will be welcome there like a brother."

"Why did anyone leave if it is so beautiful, so wonderful?"

"Too much beauty is exhausting," said the second one. "We are not beautiful men."

"Go to sleep," said the first one. He smiled, without parting his lips. He had womanly lips that never parted much. He spoke too softly. "Maybe you'll feel better in the morning."

"I will trade with you," I said, "and you can take my mule and my hand."

"We have already traded with you, but you are too drunk to remember. It is your fault if you are too drunk to trade well, ugly bird."

Had I traded already? I ran my hands along my body but it was still mine completely. The only thing that wasn't my old self was my right hand. I shook my head, and drank more wine while the three men laughed at me. They scratched at the sides of their faces like the skin itched where it connected their faces to their scalps. They did not look so monstrous. They looked like friends, to me, with such happy faces, smiling at their camp drunk.

I had more wine, and more wine.
When I woke up, I was in a desert
and a lizard ate part of my chin
and nothing I had was of my old
self.

~~~

I will trade you with you, gods and
goddesses of wherever I am. I will
trade anything I have left that is
mine. Maybe all I have left are
these words lost to the wind and
the sand.

Will you take these words and free
me from this dry, blistering land?

I will wander always north to
Valion. My people are strong, even
if the legs wear down. My hand is
old and knows the way. I will go
north, drinking my own sweat and

blood to keep it in my body and when I finally arrive among my people no one will want my ruined skin. No one will want to trade for my worn down legs. I must have already lost my beautiful eyes. I think they took everything from me when I was drugged. They must have. I am all the cast away parts of old men's pieces and a chewed upon chin that will always be scarred until it is discarded somewhere upon a dying man's face when he could not keep himself alive. No one will want to lay with me above a vineyard and watch the bees sip upon our perfumed and salted bodies.

Past the mountains, until the sun falls away from the world, there is a place where I will be one of many, in a city that knows nothing of mermaids.

When I arrive, I will offer everyone
I meet this old hand that always
knows the north star. I must lose
this hand there.

I will tell them of the travelers,
and of my mother.

If I am very lucky, I will trade
myself away entirely, until I am
scattered out into the city, and I no
longer have to carry all this pain
that I know. Let us all carry it. Let
the whole city carry pieces of this
traveler's pain, that they may
know what it means to live and die
like this, never knowing what it
means to live in a place worthy of
the name of *home*.

I sing into the sand.

Lady or the Tiger, Death Mask and Eulogy, and Other Re-Imaginings

I pray into it.

I stand up, now.

PARADISE IS A PUSH

From the arroyo side behind my
sister's house, I climbed a ladder to
cull the tops of the boxwood hedges
that were out of reach from her
yard. Two different worlds pushed
against the bent, old backyard
fence. On the one side, the
backyard, lush with rose bushes,
foreign plants like vining jasmine,
an empress tree from China, and
peaches, begonias, grass and grass
and scrub grass and clover and
grass...

The dog rules the yard, pushing a

soccer ball into the corners of everything, pushing out of the corners. This is a paradise. The neighbor has palm trees that shade the yard, as tall as clocktowers. On the arroyo side of the back fence, there's burrs, stinging weeds, hard-edged sunflowers and more burrs. The mosquitoes thrive. The biting flies and ants clamber all over. I'm climbing up to get to the boxwoods from the other side of the fence.

From the arroyo side, on the step-ladder, I can see the whole neighborhood, green behind their fences with grass, trees, beautiful decks and patio furniture. On my side, the arroyo side, there's graffiti spray-painted along a fence. A wild animal painted it in the night, marking the line between what is and is not.

Weeds are sneaking into the fence

line. On second look, the grass I just mowed isn't just grass. It's green, but it isn't grass. It's only weeds that look like grass, and some of them are getting bigger. Some of them are climbing up the sides of the house, and pushing through the slats of the fence and biting into the ground. They're sneaking in. They're taking what they can from the hot summer brown patches.

If we left this house alone for fourteen years, if this neighborhood walked out and down into the dry creek, and down to where the water pools into a small pond wrapped in brown, tall grass and dragonflies and small toads and snakes and the long, lingering, cautious look from the coyotes that live out there...

All paradises push. I'm ripping the weeds up. I'm pulling away invasive ivies. I'm back there, clipping the boxwoods.

These mountains we make that
line the street valleys, these
mountains we light up with
Christmas lights, street lights, and
headlights, rolling over the ground
like slow magma, push back.

We flew home on an airplane. The
ground is always leveled along the
airports. The ground is kept clear
and close-cropped. So much ground
leveled into a desert around the
palacial terminals. I leaned back
and imagined riding a canoe down
the arroyo, down to the river, down
to the ocean, out to sea.

I imagine heaven is a place where
the suburban sprawl is immense.
All paradises must push. New
people coming in from all over, and
there's got to be more room.

There's new houses coming up.
There's always new houses coming

up. There's new stripmalls all over.

Paradise is a push

FATHER

No, I don't want to talk about it. I
don't have to.

I fucking broke my knuckles and
I'd appreciate it if you left me
alone.

I don't care who you are.

No, I'm not hurt anywhere else.
I'm fine, you know, except that I,
you know, broke my knuckles and
I'm in excruciating pain and all,

but no I'm really fine and I'd like
you to leave. I don't want to talk to
you. Where's my mom? Did you
call her? Get her in here and get
the hell out. You don't even know
how he's doing, do you? You have
no idea. I mean, I must've busted
his nose. I know I busted his nose.
How many teeth did he lose? You
don't know? If you don't know,
then get out because I don't want
to talk to you.

I mean it.

Look, I said I don't want to talk to
you.

Yeah, I busted him up. What's it
to you? He's not gonna press
charges.

Because I know he's not.

I just do, okay.

Get off my back! Go bug somebody
else! This is none of your business.
It's between me and him and I
think you should leave.

I'm asking you nicely to please
leave, okay?

What do you mean I have to talk
to you?

But there isn't any abuse! Look at
my hands and look at his face and
tell me if there's abuse. If
anything, there's parent abuse.

So what?

Tell me how he is and then come back, okay? Find out how he's doing and then come talk to me and I'll consider your offer.

You can't do that.

No, you can't. There isn't any abuse at all! You can't do that!

Fine, you want to know what happened that badly. Fine. FINE! I'll tell you. I came home late and beat up my Dad. That's what happened. Go write up your stupid reports, and leave us the hell alone.

What do you mean? No way. No.

Look, lady, you can't do that.
Nothing happened, alright? It was
just a stupid fight. It's totally over,
totally completely over and it will
never happen again.

You can't do that! You don't
understand!

Look, I came home past curfew
and Dad and Terri got pissed.
They waited up for me and I came
home, and I thought they'd be
asleep. They weren't. They wanted
to talk about it, and I got pissed
off. I mean, I'm sixteen years old
and I don't think being out late is
such a big deal but apparently I'm
mature enough to drive, but not
mature enough to go to a few
parties now and then. So, I got
pissed and I just left. I went to my
room and locked my door and told
my dad to piss off. He broke my

door down, and I took a swing at him and now we're in the hospital and I really would appreciate it if you went to check on my Dad. I know I broke his nose pretty bad and I know his eye didn't look that good, and I know he got some teeth knocked out. I didn't want to do that to him, but he made me.

He did make me.

Yes, he did. He actually did make me do it.

Who started it? What are you talking about? There wasn't a fight. I just hit him.

Well, I lied, alright. I mean, geez, you won't even go find out about my Dad. How's he doing?

Well what's the last thing you heard?

That's great. You don't know anything. You come talk to me and you don't know a goddamn thing.

He did make me.

He told me to hit him.

I'm not lying. Really, he told me to hit him. I mean, I took the first swing and that one was all me, but after that he just kept telling me to hit him.

He did. I mean, he broke down my door and told me never to walk away from him. He was all like,

"Never walk away from me, boy.
You never walk away from me! I
am your father and you never walk
away from me!"

 That was kind of during, actually.
He said it while he was kicking
down my door, and he was still
yelling about it on the way in.
That's when I took a swing. I
busted him right in the jaw as
hard as I could. He didn't fall over
or anything, he just stumbled back
and looked real surprised. I
thought I was dead. I mean, you
know, he's a big guy. He used to
play football and stuff just like me.
He even boxed heavyweight once.
He's, like, huge. Well, I hit him
and he kinda stumbled back. I
looked at him right then and he
was just really really huge. God, I
thought I was dead. I thought he
was gonna just kill me. He looked
so shocked. I mean, he just looked
like he was, you know, really
surprised and stuff. He just, well,

he just looked at me like that. If he hadn't looked so surprised I might've hit him again.

You wanted to know so bad, well I'm telling you so shut up, lady. Don't interrupt me again with that BS. I'm telling the truth so stop twisting my words around. This is what happened next. He took off his glasses, his watch, his shirt. He even took off that necklace Terri got him in Costa Rica. He even took off his wedding ring. He took everything off. Terri came running up because it got real quiet, but she just stood in the doorway. She didn't say anything. I mean, this was about us, you know, about me and him.

Dad looked right at me and I was stepping back because I thought he was gonna open up on me. I really believed I was totally dead. He never hit me. Not even once. He just looked at me and he said, "You want to hit me, huh? You want to hit me in the face. Fine. Hit me."

I didn't even try. I thought he was gonna just use it as an excuse to get me on my feet so he could kill me. He shook his head at me like he was disappointed. He said, "I won't fight back. You have my word, boy. I won't lift a finger to stop you. I won't fight you. I can't fight you. Now get up. You want to hit me. So hit me. I'm not asking you boy. I'm telling you. Hit me."

I figured I'd rather go down on my feet. That's really what I thought. I mean, I thought he was still just playin' with me and he was gonna break me in half. I figured if I was gonna die, I'd wanna at least get one more good shot in. So I stood up and I popped him in the gut. He doubled over a little and laughed, "No, boy. You wanted to hit me in the face. You didn't want to hit me in the gut. The face, boy. Hit me right in the face."

Well, yeah. I did. I hit him right in the face. I was still pretty pissed so I was still swingin' good. I mean, I was half expecting him to turn around on me and let it loose on me, but he didn't. He'd take the shot and he'd look me in the eye and say, "Hit me again, boy. One more time." He kept saying it over and over again. I mean, I was okay with it until he started bleeding. I'll admit it. I really was. I mean, I'd been wantin' to hit him for a while. Then he started bleedin'. Didn't take long for that. Couple minutes at most, you know. He just started bleedin' every time I hit him. It was his nose first. God, I busted his nose real bad. He even

fell over for that one. That was the
first time he fell over. Then he
stood up, takin' his time to get up
and stuff and he said, "Again, boy.
C'mon. You're not done yet."

I was like, "You're bleeding."

He said, "So what? Didn't stop you
before. It's my blood. You don't
think it's your blood, do you? It's
mine. I don't care if I lose a little
blood. Hit me again. Hit me again,
goddammit. That's an order, boy.
Hit me again."

So I kept hitting him. He started
falling over a lot, but he kept
getting back up. I mean, he just
wouldn't let me stop. He just kept
getting up. What was I supposed to
do? God, I started throwing up all
over my room and he just told me
to hit him again. God, his face was

messed up. He was bleeding everywhere. His nose was fucked up. And I tried to go easy on him but he wouldn't let me. He said, "You fuckin' call that a punch? Didn't I teach you to punch better than that? What a wuss. You're a wuss, boy. You can't finish what you started. C'mon. Again. Hit me again, for real this time."

I broke my knuckles sometime after the first half hour, I think. We went at it for over two hours. He just wouldn't let me stop. He kept getting up. I mean, I didn't want to, but he kept getting up. He'd just spit the teeth out into his hand and put them in his pocket. Blood was everywhere. God he must've lost gallons of blood. I'm feeling sick, lady. I think I'm gonna puke again. That's what happened, alright.

What do you mean when did we stop? We stopped when he said I could stop. It was right after I switched hands. I hit him on the forehead and he fell over, and something snapped real loud in my hand. He stood up real, real slow - he'd been falling and standing up real slow every time - and he looked me in the face and he said, "How's your hand?"

I was holding my hand by then. I mean, I've really screwed up my knuckles. I told him, "It hurts like a motherfucker."

"Use your other hand," he said.

I said, "No. You made your point. I'm sorry. God, I'm so sorry."

He said, "Hit me again, boy.

You're not done yet. You haven't finished the job. Use your other hand."

So I did. I only got four shots in with my left hand before he couldn't get up. He lay there on the ground. He was just laying there on his back in a mess of blood and vomit from both of us and he just looked up at me and he said, "I reckon you're done, boy. I reckon you're done." That's it. That's what happened.

What about her? Well, she couldn't watch. She watched at first, but after the first couple shots she just left. I don't know what she was doing. Why don't you ask her?

Dad isn't the kind of guy you can really argue with once he's got his mind set on something.

Well, I helped him up, and we
went out to the kitchen. He wanted
a glass of water. He was bleeding
so much and he could barely walk.
I got him some water and he put
the cup up to his face and he
started drinking and so much of
his blood got in there he ended up
drinking more blood than water.
God, I feel sick. I don't want to talk
about this anymore, alright? I
don't want to talk about anything.
I think I'm gonna puke. Terri's
gotta be here. If Mom isn't here,
can you at least get Terri? Do you
know if my Mom's gonna be here?
Have you called her yet? I have her
number somewhere. I know Terri
knows where it is. Talk to her,
okay. I mean, Terri. Talk to Terri.
But I want to see my Mom, so get
her up here, too.

Hey, wait. Nothing's gonna happen right? I mean, tonight was bad, but like I said, it's over. You're not gonna do anything, right? Can you find out how he's doing for me? Please? I really need to know if he's gonna be okay.

SUBURBAN

I have noticed that all the roads
warp back upon themselves in a
disaster of urban planning.
Driving to new places, I often feel
like the kitten trapped in the
center of an endless tangle of yarn.
Thing is, the shops don't change --
the restaurants. I pass different
boxes and colors and letters that
are all relatively similar. The
houses in long lines and tracks are
all from the same waves of
builders, and all look like pretty
similar if you squint a little.
Painted differently, perhaps.

If I was in a bubble, or a matrix, this is kind of what it would be like. Roads looping back on themselves to maintain the illusion at the edge of the world, and quickly placed assets that convey a depth to the world without actually requiring too much in the way of total variation.

These thoughts kept me up at night. I squinted at the stars, and pondered the possibility of a glass dome. I looked upon the woods at the city limits and wondered why no walking trails continued on beyond the treeline, and why no farms or ranches extended out that way. The maps told me there were highways, but among the forested hills, and the way the roads twist around so much, it would be easy for a skilled architect to hide the illusions. If I took a compass in hand, and walked in a straight line for thirty miles, would I reach the end of the world?

How could I tell? I am trained to go
to work every morning, shop at
grocery stores and relax in
establishments that are indoors.
Even the campgrounds are
cordoned off around approved
rivers. There are wild places, but I
am not among them.

Did the ecology collapse outside
this bubble place? Did we get sent
here to save the life outside of it?
Are we experiments, studied or
forgotten.

Late at night, I walk the streets
along a path of safety lit by
strategically-placed lamps. Last
night, I saw a herd of deer grazing
in someone's yard. They were
small, no taller than my chest.
They looked at me nervously, like I
was about to chase them off my
neighbor's yard. I looked back at
them. They had huge, glassy eyes,
like black lenses. They held as still

Lady or the Tiger, Death Mask and Eulogy,

and Other Re-Imaginings

as street lamps.

PUT ALL HER THINGS IN A SACK

She was killed. She was shot by police in a drug raid. We weren't big drug users, and it isn't fair what happened, and we should probably sue the city over it because she died unarmed and terrified over half a bag of weed. Then, I was alone, and after everyone left from the funeral, I was still alone.

I couldn't leave the house because outside of the house it was like she had never existed at all.

It occurred to me that if I was ever going to recover from the loss, I'd need to put all the things left of her in my apartment into a large sack and leave them on the curb for trash pickup. No point keeping things around if they serve no purpose. That isn't true. They serve a purpose. The purpose they serve is to remind me in every room of something that is no longer mine. Without my memory, these objects would be just so much trash. One man's treasure is another man's trash.

Before I started to clean out the house, I made pad thai using a recipe handed down for generations in her family. Her mother had given it to us when we moved in together, written out on paper in her barely-legible, chicken-scratch. I knew the recipe by heart by now. I made it because it was the best thing I could make without cheese. I hadn't been to the store in a while. I was running out of things. I hated that it reminded me of her. I ate half. The rest, I threw into the sack.

The paper with the recipe was placed in the sack, next. On top of this was the last takeout we had had together still half-eaten in Styrofoam in the fridge. I hadn't touched it since you left it there. Something borrowed – something new. Then, I cleared out the kitchen. Stupid coffee mugs with sayings like COFFEE OR DEATH and IF YOU CAN READ THIS YOU'RE STANDING BETWEEN ME AND MY COFFEE. THAT'S BAD. God, I hated those stupid mugs. She thought they were funny. I didn't mind throwing them into the sack. Next, I went to the living room bookcase where all of the books she left behind were on one heavy shelf between our old yearbooks and a bible her father had given us for Christmas. All of it had to go in the sack.

The clothes that were left were next. Most of them had already been given away or taken by her mother and sister, but there were a few left that were too old or worn to bother with before. There was a desk that had all of her half-abandoned projects shoved into drawers and left in piles, letters on stationary, knitting needles and yarn. I found a box of her old IDs all the way back to junior high school in the back of one of her drawers. It took me an hour to work up the guts to stop staring at her life in a timelapse, and throw these away, too.

Everything goes in the sack.
Everything that was hers.

I ended in the bedroom. It was too
heavy to throw out, and it was
dark. I was tired, emotionally
exhausted. I left the sack where it
had ended up on my bed. I pushed
it over to one side and curled up
next to it. It was both soft and
bony with all the weird concretions
of things inside of it.

It was kind of like what sleeping
with her should have been like, if
we had actually grown old
together, that's what her body
would feel like. It would be soft
and baggy-skinned, like this. It
would seem to groan whenever I
moved in the night, from all the
worn-out things moving against

each other.

In the morning, I didn't have the heart to throw it out.

When she was still alive, I often woke before she did. I made coffee for two. I did it this morning, thinking that maybe the sack would like some. If we had grown old together, she would never give up coffee. The smell of coffee was generally what got her out of bed.

A loud, noisy thud from the bedroom, as if the whole sack had fallen through the furniture. It wasn't fallen through. I dashed back into the room. The sack had fallen off the bed. It had found some momentum from some of the accretions inside of it, and it had fallen over the side of the bed onto the floor. It lay there, like a bloated dead body.

I took the sack out to the living
room. Really, this time it would go.
I would throw it away. I poured a
cup of coffee for it, thinking maybe
it had fallen out of bed because it
was coming alive from the smell of
coffee, the way she had. I held a
cup of black coffee out to the sack,
hoping a little.

The mouth of the sack dropped
open.

I poured coffee into the sack, with
a cynical smile on my face. "Drink
up," I said.

The sack and I spent the rest of
the day together, in the living

room, watching basic cable. I
switched to shows she had liked,
and complained about them like I
had done before the shooting. It
felt good to have something to talk
to. I got some pot from the freezer.
I smoked a bowl of pot and asked
the sack if it wanted a hit.

It took a hit.

It rolled onto the couch.

God, I was so lonely after her
death. Even this was better than
being alone.

That night, I curled up with it on
the couch. It and I fell asleep
together.

It went on like this for a couple
more days. It didn't feel like
cheating on my wife, because she
was dead and this was the closest

I'd ever get to her short of digging
up her grave and licking her teeth.

I told the sack all about what
happened, and the funeral. She
had been shot in the face, and it
tore off most of her face. The
reconstruction wasn't really
possible, they said, unless they
made her look like a wax dummy. I
told them not to do it, just to keep
the coffin closed. No one should
remember a wax dummy. Her
mother never shed a tear. She took
care of everything. She hugged me
and told me to call her anytime,
that I was still her son. I should
call her.

The sack listened to me. I had
grown accustomed to the
particular way the sack was, and
our new routine. In the morning,
coffee for two. The coffee it drank

sloshed around inside of it. I
helped the sack go to the bathroom
in the afternoon. It had trouble
sitting on the toilet. What could I
do? I couldn't throw it out. I didn't
have the heart to throw out all her
things.

I smoked out with it, helping it
smoke by blowing into its mouth.
It coughed smoke. It belched
smoke. When I ran out of weed, I
thought about buying more, but
remembered how she died. I
thought I wouldn't be brave
enough to find a new dealer, stand
in some strange doorway and ask
for pot, when any minute the cops
could come tearing in, guns
blazing, trying to keep drug money
out of the hands of Mexican drug
cartels and terrorists.

I sat on the couch and looked at
the sack.

"I wish you could score some weed. She used to do that all the time for us. But, you can't do that, can you? You can't do anything. You're just a sack."

Enough was enough. She's dead.

I gathered my courage from coming down. I put the sack out on the corner for the trashman and raccoons.

A few hours later, someone rang the doorbell. The sack was at the door. It must have been moved there. I bent over to pick it up and move it back, but before I could heft it up, I noticed the mouth of the sack open, and a medium-sized bag of weed inside, resting on

broken coffee mugs and some old
clothes, released from a broken box
of junk where it had been stashed
under all sorts of useless receipts.

The sack came back inside with
me, then.

"So, this is for real?" I said, taking
a long hit from my bong with the
pot from the sack. I kissed the
sack's mouth, pouring the
marijuana smoke into it. It seemed
to shudder a little when I did that,
and get hot.

We watched television, ordered
take out, and drank coffee.

This new life only made me miss
her more.

The sack never said anything. It just accepted what I threw into it. It accepted it when, on a whim, I reached inside the sack to pull out bits of old food, or to pour the morning coffee carefully from the sack into the toilet. I wiped the sack with toilet paper, because it could not wipe itself. I flushed for it. I looked into the sack, when it's lips parted, and all the bits and pieces reminded me of my wife.

The first crisis came when we ran out of coffee. The weed was a miracle, and I hadn't tempted fate for more than that. Whatever magic empowered the sack, I knew that if it was like her, it would only be nice if it got coffee in the morning. I was responsible for getting coffee.

"I'll be back," I said. I showered

and shaved. I put on a collar shirt and nice jeans. "Just wait here, I'll be right back."

I stepped outside of the house. I blinked. It was bright outside. The store was bright, too. Everything was bright. I bought coffee. I bought frozen breadsticks. I bought cans of soup, spaghetti, and sauce. I bought her favorite ice cream.

At home, the sack had been waiting on the couch. I unloaded groceries. The sack dropped off the couch and rolled towards me.

"Don't worry, I'll get it," I said. "I'll get it. Just..."

I shook my head and blinked. The groceries went into the cupboards.

I had my back to the sack. When I
turned around again, it had made
it all the way into the kitchen.

"Oh, hey."

It's mouth was open.

"Hungry?" I made spaghetti early.
It was my favorite thing to cook. I
set it up at the table for the sack
and me. I sat there, looking at my
spaghetti, and the sack in the seat
across from me.

I forgot the cheese. I love cheese.
She loved cheese. We used to say
that if we could see our pasta,
there wasn't enough cheese on it.

The sack opened its huge, gaping mouth. The spaghetti leaked into the sack.

I didn't want spaghetti without cheese. I didn't want anything. The sack's open maw looked back at me, like it wanted to comfort me.

I crawled across the table. I opened the mouth of the sack. I crawled inside.

At first, it was difficult because of all the coffee-soaked broken mugs and clothes and books jabbing me and it was hard to breath inside the sack, but I got used to the pain in there. After a while, everything was fine.

There's a phone ringing. I don't know who it is. I don't know when the machine will pick it up. It just keeps ringing and ringing, and it's all I can do not to shout at it.

THE ROBBERY

Freedom from care. That's what
money means to me. Like if I had
the money I could do whatever I
wanted forever and nobody could
stop me, and I could leave this
place behind for something better.
The bank robber was not thinking
like I was. He was robbing us
because we had the money. He was
only thinking about getting the
money. He had a gun and a
getaway car. He was Hispanic or
he was faking a Spanish accent.
He was dressed like a business
man in a black suit. He had no
idea what he was doing to me.

"Empty the register. Fast, man, fast!" They train us to always do what the man with the gun demands.

"You honestly think this is a good idea? They're going to catch you."

"Hurry up!"

A woman screamed. People have noticed. The police are coming. I'm sure they'll be here any moment.

"I will do this that you ask me to do. I'm reaching for the register now and I'm doing this. Please, don't shoot. Listen, though. I have to know. What does this money mean to you?" I was doing what he demanded. I was emptying my register into the bag, meticulously, without moving too fast. Robbers don't like it when you move too fast.

"Shut up!" His hair was dyed black with grey at the temples. I'm sure of it. He has a Caucasian mouth, like a pudgy Matthew Perry. He was blond at the very tip of his roots. He had green eyes. They don't look like contacts.

I looked him in his eyes.

"I'm doing what you say. Return the favor. Tell me what the money means to you."

People are scared. They're trying not to move. Fight or flight doesn't work with guns. Bullets are too

strong and too fast. Hold still.
Hope he runs out of bullets before
you. Call for help who have more
guns -- the police. "Please," I said.

"Its just money. Hurry up."

He had given me a grocery bag to
fill up. It was a Whole Foods
reusable bag. He was going to do
this again; he needed a reusable
bag.

I was at the change now. I was
watching it go. Let him have it all.
"I wish you well," I said. I held the
bag out to him. " Hurry before they
catch you. Police are on the way."

He needed not to look too close. He
needed to run. He leaned over the

counter. I could smell his smell. A
fancy soap, vanilla or lavender or
something in between. It was an
odd smell for a man. I saw him
now for what I think he was: a
man in a nice hotel, visiting town,
and using nice hotel soap. A
professional bank robber, then. I
saw his clean shave, and the fine
hairs on his face. I had not moved
an inch backwards when he leaned
over the counter. He saw the
drawer, and looked up at the clock
on the wall. "Plenty of time."

I don't say anything. I fill up the
bag.

"You're the manager, right? You
count out the drawers?"

"That's right."

"Keep filling it up," he said. "Plenty more in there." He held the gun out.

I kept filling up the bag. There was nothing else I could do.

He was smirking now. His Hispanic accent was dropping away. The bag was heavy with paper. He reached for it, over the counter, and snatched it from me. "You want to know?" he said. "What this money means to me?"

"I do."

"It means I win."

The bank robber was smiling. He

turned quickly then, and surveyed
for heroism. He relaxed a little
when he saw no one even try to
run from him, or pull anything. He
held the gun out to the woman who
had screamed. She was cowering.
"Bang," he said. She didn't move a
muscle. She didn't breathe.

I moved. I stepped around the
counter. I walked behind him as he
slipped into his running car.

There were sirens coming this
way.

He looked over at me. He saluted
with his gun and revved the
engine. I stood in front of his car. I
folded my arms. I looked at him.
He held up the gun. I shrugged. He
laughed and backed up. He
swerved around me and was gone.
I walked away before the police
could find me.

Freedom is what money means to me. So I live free. My first night under a bridge a dirty man came for everything I had but I pushed him and fought him and shouted until he left and then I couldn't fall asleep again. The second night was better because I had found a bench and I could be up off the ground and no one came to chase me off. I found an apple tree in an abandoned yard after that. The fruits were small and hard and tart but I ate until I could burst. I was sick from eating all the apples I could stomach. Then, I went to the police station and no one knew what I was doing there. I gave a statement about the robbery, and how scared I was and that's why I ran away. They wrote it down. They told me to go home.

I went home and took a shower
and it was like nothing had
happened.

It was worse than being caught.

GO FORTH; BE MIGHTY

We had to drink oil, ourselves, to work there, trading some part of us in for the machines of industry. The bodmodders came to our cafe to get their whale oil fix mixed with espresso. Doppio Con Brava, or Cinnos with oil frothy from hot steam. We had to be like the customers to work there or we'd never know whether the oil had soured.

My folks were management. They supported me long enough after I flunked out of grad school to

believe that any job was good and
there was no place for pride with
some of their kids that weren't
destined for management. They
even bought my first mod so I
wouldnt go in debt to the company
store. I had my eye replaced with a
scanner so I could keep my fingers
safe from the whirring gears of the
oil machine. A couple months
later, I had enough burn scars to
give in to my boss' suggestion. I
had my fingers replaced, too. My
boss was a bastard about it before
I had it done. Speed was
everything. Accuracy and speed.
Moving bodies through the line we
were expected to besmiling to the
customers and working like
machines. Up until midnight for
the late shifters. Up again at 5:00
am for the truck loaders with
hands as thick as flippers.

My mom was worried about me all
red-eyed and metal edged, a
broken gaze when she saw me all
worn out and popping the pills and

oils that keep the machinery from rejection. I was still living with them, because I couldn't afford to move out. They tried to support me at my first job. My mom got an inner ear fix so she wouldn't need to carry her tablet to answer the phone and email. She got up with me early the next day, and drove me in for earlybird swing shift starting at 6:30. Line was out the door. I rushed in, clocked in, and jumped behind the whirring machines, grinding beans and keeping the oil hot and fluffy. Mom got up in line and saw us working. Tried to say hi to us, shake the boss's hand among the gears of the city. Boss didn't even look up. Her hands weren't any good for shaking anymore. Too much happening on the screen to stop and chat. I tried to introduce my mother to my boss, and my boss wouldn't even say hello and look my mother in the face. Got home

that night and we didn't talk about
it.

It wasn't the life she wanted for
me, but she couldn't say anything
about it because it was the life I
had. She just looked at my hands
funny sometimes and saw my
burned, oily, steel fingers like they
were an infection. I was too tired
to say anything about her implant.
I was just too tired.

There's an implant I can buy so I
can turn my sleep cycle on and off.
I've almost got enough saved up.
Trying to do it without anymore
debt. Maybe I'll get my feet next,
instead. My feet hurt all the time.

And they come all day to drink
whale oil and espresso. Work hard.
More machine than man, in debt
for the mods that pay off debts.
That's how they get you, we all
say.

"Go forth; be mighty," they told me

Lady or the Tiger, Death Mask and Eulogy,

and Other Re-Imaginings

once.

WAR BEETLES

War beetles left wreckage like
hurricanes across the plains. The
battle still raged on at some far
distant place over the horizon.
Along the ground, in their wake,
acid pooled. Smoke from the fires
of war left a gunpowder stink
hanging in the air, and all the
fresh meat of the dead made it
smell worse.

Meridian Smith, a survivor of the
battle, walked cautiously over the
devastation with a girl he had
found in a village. He had solid

boots that rode high up his legs, near to his hips, and a long duster jacket. Meridian had lost his helmet in the fight. His forehead and ears were deep red, now. He didn't think about the sunburn, though. He was too busy watching out for the ground, and for the little girl that held his hand. He had to lead her carefully, because the earth was full of holes and sinkholes and smashed bushes and the remains of animals.

Desdemona was her name, she had said. She walked beside Meridian, clinging to his hands. She wasn't brave enough to walk by herself. She was too small to traverse the fields without his strong arm lifting her over the worst of the destruction. Her shoes were not built for long travel. Meridian was surprised she hadn't complained about her feet, yet.

Desdemona's little mouth opened.
She sighed, theatrically. Meridian
had a vision of his own daughter,
in her teens, sighing all the time
over nothing. Desdemona spoke
over another sigh "Daddy?" she
said.

"Don't call me that," said
Meridian. "My name is Meridian
Smith. Stop calling me your father.
Call me Mr. Smith if you can't say
Meridian. It's what my daughter
always called me."

He lifted Desdemona over the top
of a dead war fly, bloated with pus
and sparking where the wires were
exposed in the carapace.

Desdemona had only a white lace
dress on, like a landlord's
daughter. It wasn't white,

anymore, exactly, but it used to be white. She had pink, canvas shoes. In the few hours that Meridian had pulled her out of a supply depot's tornado shelter, Desdemona's shoes had gone from pink to mud as if they had never been anything but dirty.

"I can't remember your name," said Desdemona. "It's too long."

"Call me Mr. Smith if you can't say Meridian. You can say that, right?"

"Mr. Smith. Okay. Got it. Mr. Smith, I have to tell you something."

"What?"

"I have to pee."

"Then find somewhere to pee. I'll wait." Meridian tried to let go of her hand.

She clung to it. She grabbed Meridian's hand in both of hers, and pulled on him. "No!" she shouted. "Don't let go!"

"Can you pee if you're holding my hand?"

"No," she said. "Not with people looking. Not with people around."

"Then you have to let go."

"Okay," she said. "Mr. Smith, I'm hungry, too." She still hadn't let go of Meridian's hand.

"We don't have anything to eat right now," said Meridian. "Sorry."

It took Desdemona a long time to let go of his hand. When she did, at last, she carefully picked her way to the back of a hunk of broken off war beetle, the size of a dead buffalo. It was the only privacy apparent, here. When she finished, she cried out and held up a hand. Meridian walked back to her. He picked her up and over the bleeding wreckage.

"I didn't wash my hands," she said.

"That's okay, just this once," he said. Meridian scanned the horizon. If the war beetles turned back this way, with the fight, Meridian and Desdemona would be crushed. The beetles were moving fast, though, and they were being chased all the way by the other army's air force of automata and chimaeras.

Meridian touched Desdemona's arm, above her wrist. It felt cold. He wondered if she might die in the night of hypothermia. It got windy on the plains. He would have to give her his duster after dark. He started walking. She laughed, and said he was her pet beetle, not the other way around.

"What do you know about beetles, Desdemona?" said Meridian. "I'm not a beetle."

"We have toy beetles," she said.

"And little beetle riders. They grow war beetles from eggs as big as grapefruits. Some of them fly. War beetles are the biggest of the biggest. They're mean and want to eat your face."

"They are big," said Meridian. "They get giant fast, too. They only live about forty years, and they just keep growing."

"Beetles make the best pets. My sister had a pet beetle that looked like a girl except when she was naked. She had to go away, though."

Meridian was only half-listening. He was just glad the kid wasn't crying or throwing fits. He'd agree with anything she said. "The wonders never cease," said

Meridian. "I've only seen the big ones. I'm not from around here. We have different kinds of beetles."

"Like what kind?"

"Well, like little ones that get really, really big, until they're so big they want to eat you."

Meridian couldn't tell if the spurt of cloud in the distance was acid smoke or something worse.

"Why do they want to eat you?"

"They're hungry. They aren't smart, either."

"But why?"

"Don't start that."

Perhaps it was smoke, and a war beetle had been gutted open by its enemy, roasted by its own burst acid sacs, spilling toxic fumes into the clouds that would poison anyone caught in the breeze of it.

"Start what?"

"Be quiet a while, Desdemona. I have to think."

"Okay."

He tried to move faster away from the suspicious clouds.

They reached a new town by late
afternoon. It had been flattened
and burned just like Desdemona's.
Meridian had never seen so much
wasted chitin. It took forever to
grow in a mold, and there it all
was, lying in the street in strips
and fragments. At least this town
didn't have much acid scarring.
The war beetles had slowed down
long enough to level the town, then
moved on. That meant there might
be food, and new clothes. Meridian
needed to change if he wanted to
get all the way west. He was
wearing the wrong uniform.

Meridian stopped at some mostly
smooth chitin that had been
knocked into the middle of the
main street. He pulled Desdemona
down off his back onto the plank.
The chitin was a beautiful black
pearl that must have cost someone
a fortune to import. It was mostly

flat, with a very subtle curve that made an adequate, clean spot for a little girl to sit and rest.

"You stay here," said Meridian.

"I don't want to," she replied. She folded her arms and pouted.

"I mean it," said Meridian. "If you move from this spot before I get back, I will not come and get you. You will be on your own. You stay right here, until I get back. Got it?"

Her eyes opened up. "Don't leave me," she said.

Meridian felt terrible because of the lie. She had believed him, and it was for her own good that he had done it. If she survived long enough, she'd grow to hate him like his own daughter had. It was better to lie. The last thing he needed was a little girl with lockjaw or cuttle fever from all this jagged metal and chitin.

He still felt bad for lying. It reminded him of home. He tried to smile encouragingly. "Why don't you sing a song to pass the time?"

"I don't know any songs," she said.

"Make one up if you have to. I bet you have a pretty voice."

She scrunched her face into a mean glare. There would be no singing this day.

Meridian Smith unsheathed an electric knife from his left boot. He went to work on the side of the depot. The building had been leveled like a smashed potato, but there was probably a basement storage intact with dry goods. Too many tornadoes roamed the plains, so everyone had a basement. That's how Meridian had found Desdemona, while he was scrounging for food one town back.

Meridian looked at the mess everywhere, for anything that looked like it was still sealed and safe to eat. He didn't see any canned goods or boxes. He saw lots of fresh vegetables that had been left in the wreckage. It would be too risky to eat with any biological warfare from the breathing ventricles of the war beetles. If this town had been flattened by cavalry beetles, the vegetables were probably safe. If the town had been flattened by the really big, horned beetles, nothing was safe.

"Hello!" he shouted, into the black void. "Anyone down there?"

The room echoed back Meridian's own voice. At least that meant there was a large room down there, like a cavern, probably with shelves that probably had dry goods that hadn't been crushed under a two-story chitin building. If the building had caved, there'd be no echo.

Meridian turned around to check on Desdemona. She sat with her hands around her ankles and her head pressed into her knees. She was exactly where he had left her, in the exact posture. She stared at him from between her knees.

"Hey, Mr. Smith, did you find anything good?" she said. "More war beetles?" Her face lit up with fear.

"No, of course not!" said Meridian. He pointed up at the sky. "I'm worried about thunderstorms. We don't have hats or umbrellas. You keep an eye out for any clouds you see, okay? Especially purple clouds. Those are the worst storms. If you see one, you shout about it, okay?" He still felt awful for lying to a child

She didn't stand up. But she nodded, and bit her lip like she was looking very hard. She shielded her eyes with one hand,

and scanned the skyline. "I don't see any storm clouds," she said.

"You just keep looking for me, okay?"

"Okay, Mr. Smith."

Meridian cut around the hole he had made in the chitin floor tiles. He could fit an arm through now, if he tried. He didn't have a flashlight. He had kept most of his supplies in his rucksack, which hadn't survived the flying moth's acid bombs. He was lucky he had an electric knife with a fresh charge.

When he thought he had a big enough hole, he turned off his knife and sheathed it back into the top of his boot. He stripped off his

filthy duster, and slithered his
lanky body down into the gap in
the chitin.

When he landed, he heard a splash
at his feet, and a hiss like two
snakes. His boots didn't feel
steady. The smell in the air was
frightening and familiar.

He jumped up fast and tugged
himself out of the hole he had cut
as quickly as he could. He ripped
his boots off, without touching the
bottoms, and buried them in dust.

The heavy boot soles simmered
like strips of bacon.

A war beetle had shoved a trunk
into the basement and dropped an

acid bomb, to kill anyone that had been hiding. Some beetle rider was probably feeling proud of himself for thinking of that trick.

Beetle acid was engineered to be a trap. You could only smell it if you broke the surface tension. Even then, you had to know the smell to get out in time. Puddles of acid could lie simmering slowly in a hole for a decade, eating the insects that thought to lay eggs there. During the trek overland from Desdemona's destroyed town, they had to walk around whole ponds of acid, and watch for the spurts of it that had pooled in the low places in the grass, dripping off the backs of enemy beetles.

Meridian looked over at the girl, unmoved on the broken roof of chitin.

"I can't go anywhere until my boots stop cooking," said Meridian. "Mind if I join you?"

Desdemona shrugged.

Meridian sat down on the far side of the chitin wall, right on the edge. He stretched his feet out in front of him. "I never wear socks," he said. "I've got big, stinky feet." He wiggled his grubby toes.

Meridian pulled his left leg up to his nose. He gave his toes a big whiff and gasped at the stench. He rolled his eyes like marbles and sputtered for air, flailing one arm around while clutching at his throat with the other.

Desdemona smirked, but only a little.

That was something, at least.

"You know, I didn't find anyone down there," said Meridian.

Desdemona pointed. "What happened to your boots?"

Meridian turned around and looked at the footwear, lying in a pile of dust, still smoldering a little. He had only been in the acid a moment, and he hadn't lingered long. The stitching was thick. The soles were made of rubber and chitin. The steel toes and the thick, cow leather should survive a quick splash.

Meridian smiled. "My toes are too stinky," he said. "My boots needed a break from the smell. Otherwise, the stink starts to wear down the boots. Terrible, really. My daughter... I have a daughter who's all grown up, now... Well, she said she could smell my feet even if I was wearing socks and sitting on the other side of the room. I'm giving my boots a break to recover."

He rubbed the back of his head.

"Where are we going to go next?" said Desdemona. She let go of her own legs. She straightened her knees, and leaned backwards. She adjusted herself with her hands from side to side as if her legs had fallen asleep holding so still on the hard chitin.

Meridian scanned the horizon for signs of trouble.

"We'll go on to the next town. We have to be careful, though. Tornadoes and thunderstorms will be looking for us."

"I wish I had an umbrella," she said. "A really big one. Yellow."

"Is that your favorite color?"

"No way. That's a boy's color. My favorite color is pink."

"Why not have a pink umbrella?"

"You're taller than me. You have to

carry the umbrella, or you'll get wet. The umbrella should be yellow."

"You know what, Desdemona? I think you're right. A big, yellow umbrella would be just the thing for us."

Meridian rubbed his forehead, then winced and pulled his hand away. He had forgotten he was sunburned. He looked at the sky, where the sun was hanging about at 16:30, late afternoon.

Desdemona pulled her knees back to her face, and hugged her shins. "I'm really hungry," she said. "How come I can't call you daddy, Mr. Smith?"

"You already have one of those, don't you?"

"I thought every grown-up was a daddy."

"I'm not your daddy, though. Don't you have your own parents?"

"I've had a few. The first ones were nice, but then I didn't like them very much. The second ones were mean and always took me to church. I had another mommy. She was okay, but she didn't like me. I ran away. Now I have you."

Meridian pondered her words carefully. "I see," he said, slowly, though he did not understand her. "I'm not your daddy. I'm only a daddy to one person, and she never calls me that."

"Why not?"

He thought for a moment about telling her the truth. Instead, he said, "You know, my daughter only calls me Meridian Smith, or Mr. Smith. Sometimes she calls me other things, but she never calls me 'Daddy'."

"Why not?"

"That's a good question. I guess you'll have to ask her if you meet her."

"When will I meet her?"

"Never, if you're lucky."

"Why can't I meet her?"

Meridian looked over at his shoes.
They were still smoldering a little,
but they could use some more dust
to take the worst of the acid.

"Let me get back to you on that
one," he said.

He hopped off the broken wall, and
walked to his boots. He pounded
them around in the dust. He kept
at it until the burning rubber
smell dissipated. He pulled them
on carefully, ready to yank his foot
out if he felt even the slightest
touch of acid. The boots were fine.
He walked back to Desdemona,
and couldn't help but feel like
there were rocks stuck to the
bottom of his boots. His hips had
the awkward feeling of

unevenness. He needed new boots, now, among everything else.

There wasn't anything he could do about his broken boots now, and he was still better off with the boots on than walking over the wreckage all around with nothing but bare feet.

"Listen, Desdemona, we're going to look around town and see if we can find something good to eat. It has to be something in a box or a can. It has to be sealed up tight before we open it. We can't eat anything that was left lying around, like those vegetables at the depot, okay?"

She made a gagging sound in her throat. "I don't like vegetables."

"Good, because I forbid you to eat them. Fruits are right out of the question, too. No vegetables, and no fruit. We will only eat our favorite things, in boxes and cans."

Meridian scanned the horizon again, always watching out for signs of beetles in the distance, those war machines racing furiously across the chessboard, to flank and kill other beetles, other moths, other cities.

He and Desdemona were going to have to spend the night where they were, no matter what. They were safer in a town — even a ruined one — than they would be out on the plains. There were fewer wild scavengers, and they could pick through the domiciles for better clothes for Desdemona. She wasn't dressed for traveling. Meridian needed boots, a change out of his soldier's clothes. They'd have to find somewhere low in case the war came back. Harder to get tramped if they were already underground.

If they were lucky, they'd find a house with a basement that hadn't gotten an acid bath when the beetles destroyed everything, and wouldn't need an electric knife to open up. They could hide in deep shelter until morning.

The road curved through the ruined city. Puddles of acid had accumulated in ditches and gutters. Meridian was careful to hold Desdemona's hand, and lead her as far away from any suspicious puddles as he could.

The domiciles this close to the main road were small, cheap things. Laborers and field hands lived in these houses in handfuls and bunches, piled up in bunk beds. If these buildings had had basements, they probably hadn't had big ones, and they probably hadn't kept anything there but heaps of their vile hemp-soma.

The piles of wreckage were slightly more substantial a few roads over, which indicated wealthier domiciles. Meridian led Desdemona between two large piles carefully, always watching where she stepped for anything that might cut through her shoes. Kids never had decent shoes. They outgrew them too quickly. Her shoes already looked like they wouldn't last another day of hard travel.

Meridian stopped suddenly. He heard the familiar clicking and sliding sound of a shotgun swallowing shells, getting ready to spit them out with a bang. Meridian spun fast towards the sound of the gun, but too late to do anything. He yanked Desdemona behind him, clinging to her hard with one hand so she didn't fall into anything, and didn't sneak out from behind his body.

A middle-aged man in overalls had been hiding in the shadows of wreckage. He slowly lifted his shotgun. The tip of his shotgun was just past Meridian's arm length. The man had been very good to get so close to Meridian, while Meridian was distracted by Desdemona.

Meridian yanked hard on

Desdemona's hand. She was off-
balance, and it hurt her to be
tossed around and held like that,
flailed like a fish on a line. She
made pathetic whimpering noises,
oblivious to the danger of the gun.

"Howdy," said the man with the
shotgun. "You lost your helmet,
huh? Wonder what kind of head-
piece you had. Was it a big helmet,
like the moth scouts, or was it one
of them brain-implanting numbers
the war beetles use?"

Meridian was used to lying to
grown men, but he knew he
couldn't lie to this man. This man
was clean among the ruins, with
white skin as pure as milk. He was
hiding among larger, wealthier
domiciles. He was a quiet stalker,
accustomed to hunting trophy
animals. He was a landowner. He
was not some numb laborer

blissing on hemp-soma. This man had even recognized Meridian Smith's uniform.

"I lost my beetle in the first assault," said Meridian, telling the truth. "I was out on the open plains when I lost my beetle. I think I was the first casualty, too. I didn't do this to your city, or to anyone's. I barely ejected with my life. I'm just a deserter, walking west." Meridian felt strange, lying to a child all day, then telling the truth to an adult.

"You've got a toy there, too," he said.

"I found Desdemona in a basement when I was looking for food. I couldn't leave her there. Look, don't shoot me, okay? I'm not looking for trouble."

Desdemona was sobbing now,
screaming with her pain and fear.

The man with the shotgun spoke
over her wails. "If you think I'm
going to let you live just because I
might accidentally hit your little
toy..."

"I've been looking for survivors.
The plains aren't safe. We can
make it to the west border, cross
into the swamps. We'll all be
refugees together there, and there
won't be any difference between
us. We'll be safer there than here."

He spit. "Safe until the war beetles
turn that way."

"You've got a steady hand with that boomstick," said Meridian. "You ever killed a man?"

"You have," he said. He leveled his gun. He was steeling his will to pull the trigger on his first human being and his hands weren't even trembling.

Meridian's first battle, years ago, he was sweating so hard he lost control of the beetle where it interfaced at his temples. Commanders shouted angrily for seven long minutes in the middle of close combat, while nothing was wrong on the dials, but nothing was working. Meridian took his helmet off to check the interface, and saw all that damp sweat gumming up the fungal inserts. He had dropped his helmet from trembling hands three times before he had cleared the sweat.

This man with the overalls and the
shotgun was probably a good,
brave man. If Meridian moved
fast, he'd be shot. If it was a rifle
or a handgun, Meridian stood a
chance, but a spray of pellets
meant he'd be cut down like
ground beef before he'd even have
his knife unsheathed.

He clutched Desdemona's hand
hard. She whimpered. "Wait," said
Meridian. "Just take Desdemona. I
don't want her to get hurt."

The man cocked his head. "You
crazy? I've got children to bury!"

"Just wait one minute!" Meridian
said. "Take Desdemona, and hide
her eyes. She's been through

enough. She's seen enough.
Please?"

He smiled with his mouth. His
eyes never lost their deadly focus.
"Fine," he said. "You send her on
over, then."

Meridian let go of Desdemona's
hand. She held onto his, hard. He
lifted her up like a doll. She was so
light. He held her up in the air.
She was smiling at him, as if he
really was her daddy.

"Desdemona, you have to go with
this man."

"I don't want to, Mr. Smith."

"Do what I say," he said. "Go."

"Is he going to be my new daddy?"

"I don't know, Desdemona. Just go to him, for now, okay?"

Her hands let go. She wasn't strong at all. She was light, too, and not hard to hold.

Meridian pulled his hand in close and shoved into a jacket pocket. His other hand, he placed on the pommel of his electric knife at the top of his boot. It was out in the open. The landowner could see it.

Desdemona reached up for Meridian. He lifted a boot and pushed her with his foot, gently, towards the man with the shotgun.

She stood just under the barrel of
the gun, looking at Meridian with
those sad eyes that all children
seemed to have mastered the
moment they were born.

Meridian felt a lump in his throat.
He choked it down. He didn't want
to cry in front of her. He wanted
her not to see what was going to
happen. "Desdemona, why don't
you go look around the corner, see
if you can find a storm."

The landowner spit out of the side
of his mouth. It was blood, from
somewhere inside. "Go on, and get
out of here. Don't look back."

"You go over to that man, and you
listen to him," said Meridian. "He's
going to take good care of you."

"Is not," she said. "He's mean." She took a step back towards Meridian.

"You're better off with him than you are with me right now."

"Why?" She reached out to Meridian with tiny, beautiful hands.

"Because I'll be too dead to help you."

"Why?" She took another step. Her eyes clouded with tears,

"Because he's going to kill me."

"But why?!" Her voice cracked with

her wails.

The man with the shotgun lowered his weapon to Desdemona.

Meridian breathed in. He raised a hand. He couldn't imagine such an act fast enough to try and stop it in time.

The man in overalls pulled a trigger. Desdemona took one barrel in the back of the head, point blank.

Desdemona's head opened up like fireworks. She had been part beetle, part machine. None of her was really a girl. Bits of chitin and plastic and metal bounced like shrapnel off Meridian's tall boots.

Some of the shot busted through
the plastic brainpan, gears and
pumps inside Desdemona's head.
The shot peppered Meridian's
thighs like strong insects, but they
didn't draw much blood after
busting through so much hard
chitin.

Desdemona's joints spasmed, and
then stiffened. She fell like a tree
trunk. Golden lubricants from the
pneumatic tubes in her neck
spurted on the grass as if to a
heartbeat pulsing in her chest — a
mechanical heart, in a mechanical
chest.

"Dumb toys," said the man with
the gun. "My daughter had one.
Drove me nuts." He lifted the
weapon up again, to Meridian's
chest.

Meridian's knife was in his hand the moment of the blast. His face was pale and shocked and his lips trembled with the beginning of tears, but he was still a soldier. He had driven the mighty war beetles, had merged with their primitive minds, to tear down enemy cities, and he had poured death upon the enemy where his commanders had aimed the herd. Meridian's face was shocked, but his knife was out and on. It hummed in his palm like a ritual chant.

Meridian feinted left. The man with the shotgun took the bait, fired into air, hitting only the long duster coat, a small bit of shoulder, and the space where Meridian Smith was mostly not. Meridian whipped around to the right, knocked the shotgun up, and stepped behind the man's back. Meridian's electric knife hummed

in the air next to the man's throat.
Meridian pulled the spent double-
barrel shotgun out of the man's
hands. The gun clattered
somewhere behind them.

Meridian stood there, holding the
humming knife at the terrified
man's throat. Meridian stared at
Desdemona's flickering wires and
churning gears. They slowly
wound down in the grass between
the wrecked domiciles.
Desdemona's interior plastics and
casements reminded Meridian
Smith of his war beetle's chitin
and steel, when it had been sliced
open by lucky moth bombers. The
beetle was the first casualty in the
first assault of this young war. The
primitive mind of the beetle,
connected directly into Meridian's
brain, screamed in agony until
Meridian turned off the creature's
pain receptors. If Meridian had
ejected instead of easing the
beetle's pain, Meridian would have

been able to save his rucksack, with all his survival gear. Before he unplugged his helmet and ejected, he even took a long moment to read the beetle's mind, as clear without pain as if everything was fine. The creature felt gaps in its body that didn't hurt anymore, as if such things were perfectly natural. All things are perfectly natural to war beetles as long as those things didn't cause them pain. The beetle prodded the burning breeches with its own weakening limbs and trunks. It wondered how such a change had happened so suddenly, and wondered what kind of creature it would become next, as if it was to molt its shell as it had when it was young, growing to this enormous size. Was it to become smaller, this time?

The way Desdemona's gears and

wires rolled down to stillness was
like the way the beetle had died,
slowly winding down. She probably
wondered what had happened, and
what was going to happen. Yet,
she was stuck inside the shell of
innocence that had been designed
for her by the people that had
engineered the girl out of the
carapace.

Meridian Smith hadn't known the
truth about Desdemona. He would
never truly know.

KING BASILISK'S PALACE

We were headed for King Basilisk's Palace, and we knew it. All of us knew it. When the boat stopped, we knew.

The prison ship guards chained us all in a long line before we were brought above deck. I was pulled from my cage and chained up like any of the men. I felt them all – guard, prisoner - pulling on the chains, and all the bodies pulling up and down the line. I heard the weak footsteps of the prisoners. I heard their breathing. I saw only the dark of the prisons.

The guards were tribesmen from
the upper Nile that had followed
the river out to sea. They were
known to us in the ports of
Antioch. I could smell the dirty
saltwater of their skin. They
reached into my cage, and I could
strike at them because of the
smell. They didn't say anything
about it that I understood. They
barely spoke the languages of the
civilized world. One of them knew
my name and muttered at me, No,
Rebecca... but it sounded wrong to
me. When they came below deck to
chain us up, they spoke with their
whips and their shoves. These
were more effective than their
mangled words. I was chained up,
with the rest of the prisoners. It's
hard to fight back when you're
blind.

I hadn't been out of my cage in a month, and I had trouble standing up straight. I wasn't the only one. I heard men howling all around me at aches and pains from our long sea voyage. I heard the sound of whips, and the heavy boots that meant a guard was near me. Prisoners didn't have boots.

The guards dragged us up onto the deck. We fell all over each other. The guards didn't mind whipping us to our feet. I heard someone laughing. I don't know if it was a guard or a prisoner. It was just laughter, in between all those whip cracks and pained groaning of men moving for the first time in weeks.

I saw light. I had forgotten what it was like to stand in daylight, with the milk-colored sunlight pushing through my cataracts. I was happy

to see the light, even if that meant
we had finally reached King
Basilisk's city.

I don't know where the guards
took us. We walked down a long
plank. We walked over dirty
streets and stumbled over trash.
People in the city around us threw
things at us. I closed my eyes and
walked. I couldn't see anything
well enough to dodge. All I could
see was sunlight.

I was glad to be on land. On the
ship, I had been kept apart in a
special cage – for my own safety –
but that didn't stop men from
throwing things through the bars,
and urinating towards me. If the
motion of the waves moved me too
close to the edge of the cage, I
knew palms would reach for me. If
my food arrived, I knew things
were missing.

What did comfort and security
matter to us, the walking stones?
The other prisoners were silent
now. Some of them were weeping
quietly. I could hear them. Most of
them were silent. We had plenty of
time to accept our fate at sea, if we
could accept it. If not, we had time
to finish weeping before port.

We walked uphill a long time. I
imagine they could have hired us
into a cart of some kind, but they
probably wanted us tired at the top
of the hill, where King Basilisk
waited for his stones. We had
people all around us, throwing
trash at us.

I don't know when we reached our
destination. I saw only light and
shadow. I couldn't smell anything

chained to other dirty prisoners.
The road felt the same under my
feet. I don't know when we crossed
over to the palace yard. The world
became quiet around us. The wind
picked up.

Eventually, we stopped.

Men murmured and someone
screamed before someone else
could strike him quiet. A loud
stone gate pounded shut behind
us. A small wooden gate opened
gently ahead of us. Then the real
screaming started.

The chains pulled every which
way. I fell down, with my hands
above me, jerked around as if
between a dozen fish on a dozen
fishing lines. It hurt. My head
banged on a rock, and tears
pushed through my broken eyes.

Screaming dwindled. Whimpering
remained. Heavy footsteps – King
Basilisk himself, I presumed –
paced closer towards me on careful
cat feet. Huge cat feet. A shadow
fell over the light in my face.

His voice was like wind in a
canyon, and ponderously slow.
You're blind, he said, softly. Your
eyes are milky cataracts. They're
not supposed to send me the blind.

I turned my face to the sound of
the voice. I'm... I'm sorry, I
muttered.

King Basilisk walked on from me
towards the whimpering sounds.

My chains had become very still.
All around me, men had become
stones.

I heard King Basilisk's windy
voice. It won't hurt, and you won't
truly die, he said. Please, just open
your eyes.

The whimpering voice protested.

King Basilisk spoke peacefully.
You are so afraid. Do not be. I will
not hurt you. I will calm your
fears, and end all your miseries.

Chains rattled, though I could not
feel them. Whimpering became
screaming. Screaming was sliced
out of the air as if with a sword.

King Basilisk's heavy footsteps

returned to me. Sometimes brave men pluck their own eyes out with a rock when they know they are before me. The deed usually kills these men from the bleeding. You were not brave to infect yourself with the cataracts, were you?

No, my lord, I said. I lost my sight before I can remember anything.

What could a blind thing like you do to deserve this fate in my palace?

Great King Basilisk, I beg of you... I fell to one knee.

His voice grew an edge like a chill in the breezy whispers. Do not beg anything of me, he said.

He pinched the chains where they
bit my wrists, and the metal bent
and snapped open.

I clasped my hands over my heart.
I whimpered. Let my death be
swift, my lord. I beg of you to let
my death be swift let me die swift
let me die swift let me die swift...

I don't know if he heard me or not.
His footsteps turned away from
me. A shadow passed over my eyes
- I imagined a frightful tail about
to smash me. Instead, the shadow
swung away. I heard King Basilisk
abandoning me in the yard. He
sounded like a cat the size of an
elephant. His gentle steps had so
much weight in them. A wooden
gate opened. Then, it closed.

I waited for the guards to come for

me. I felt around my feet, and discovered the stones wrapped in rags that used to be my countrymen, my fellow prisoners. Some of the remaining rags came loose from the men, and I wrapped them over my feet.

I waited a long time.

I fell asleep in the yard. Just before I dropped into the dreamworld, I wondered if I would ever wake up again.

It rained later. I held my mouth open and drank as much as I could catch. It wasn't a strong rain, but it was enough to cool my throat.

When the rain stopped, King Basilisk returned to me with food. I felt his gigantic claw upon my

hand, like a dog's paw seeking my
attention. It was a gentle touch,
but I felt the weight behind it, of
the huge monster. I held my
breath. I expected his claw to rip
me open. Instead, he lifted my
hand with his claw and moved it
over to rest upon a loaf of bread.

You are a woman? said King
Basilisk, with his windy voice.

I nodded, with my mouth full of
bread.

Did you kill anyone?

I shook my head. I stole things, my
lord.

Why?

I don't know, my lord.

I have nothing to steal inside these walls. What have you heard of my palace?

Your stones were men, once. All the prisoners are turned to stone. Then, you use them to build your palace, and your city walls. I broke off bits of bread, shoved them cautiously in my mouth. I wondered if the bread was poisonous. Was this to be my last meal?

King Basilisk did not speak of execution. You cannot see them, he said, but you should wonder at what it looks like, all these men caught in their moment of fear, twisting and struggling against my eyes. The Architect Guild always struggles mortaring the stones together tightly. It's gruesome to behold. Finish your bread, he said. Then, we will go for a walk.

We sat in silence while I ate. Then, King Basilisk lifted my palm with his forepaw, and me with it, to my feet. His bestial claws held my delicate hand like a miniature teacup, delicate and unbreaking. He turned and moved his body, then placed my hand on his hot side. His scales were smooth as glass. I felt like I was touching a giant lamp. Stay with me, blind one, he said.

King Basilisk walked on four legs like a lizard. One foot was directly in front of me. One was directly behind me. In between, I hurried to keep up with his slow steps. He led me to the palace wall. He took my hand again. He pressed my

body against the wall. I felt the
bumps of heads and feet and
twisting hands. I ran fingers in the
gaps where cement mortaring
found ways to hold the densely-
packed limbs together.

This was supposed to deter crime,
said the King. All these criminals
turned to stone, and anyone could
look up and see them. Do you know
what it did to us?

No, my king.

From all over the world, criminals
come. They fill my harbor. We
profit from criminals here. Our city
receives the ships full of criminals,
receives all those fees and taxes
and foreign coins. I have reigned
132 years. Generations of men
have grown up only processing

criminals for coins. The expanding
wealth of my citizens has attracted
new criminals. I wonder what
would happen to my city's wealth
if my gruesome walls truly
discouraged crime.

King Basilisk led me away from
the wall. He led me through a
door, into a palace, where no light
spilled over my face. My footsteps
echoed like tiny hail drops next to
King Basilisk's thunderous paws. I
felt no furniture in these halls. I
heard no other life but the King
and my terrified breathing.

He led me to a small garden
hidden inside the palace walls,
where light fell across my face
again. He led me to first one small
tree, then another, and both full of
ripe cherries. He showed me a
large basket, too.

For now, I want you to pick the

cherries. They have come in fine
this summer.

I fingered the ripe fruit, and the
large basket at the base of the tree.
My hunger conquered my fear.
May I eat some while I work? I
said.

Of course. There's more here than
you could possibly steal, thief.

I had to pull the cherries out by
hand. It would have been easier to
do this with a knife, but I did not
expect such a thing in my hands,
nor did I ask.

When I ran out of room in my
basket, King Basilisk was there.
(As if he never left, he was there. I

imagine him watching me in
silence and pondering my fate in
his garden.) King Basilisk told me
to carry the basket and follow his
footsteps. I was not sure where we
were going, but I followed.

You were not a very good thief, to
be caught.

No, my king.

A shame, that. When the
architects come to speak with me
and gather their stones in the
morning, they will want to kill you.
I haven't decided if I'll let them.

I said nothing.

Have you ever been to Iberia?

No, my king. I was born in Antioch, and this voyage is my first beyond her walls.

He spoke slowly, even for him, as if reciting a poem from memory though his words had no rhyme or meter. I have heard stories of the mountains of Iberia, how the sunsets are every color of the rainbow, and the trees turn purple in the twilight and bow to the fey nightwalkers of the valleys. I have heard of shepherds in the hills that master music while watching their flocks of sheep. I read about a monastery at the top of a hill where wealthy consumptives seek a cure, and wealthy monks live in luxury selling a cure that never seems to come.

He led me to a room.

You can sleep here, for now. The
door doesn't lock, but the gates to
the palace will seal tight. Even if
you escaped your room, I'd find you
before you could escape the palace.
You would not get far if you did, I
assure you.

His heavy paw descended into the
basket of cherries. My load
lightened when he was done.

You can keep the rest of the
cherries, in case you hunger again.
You will work hard in the morning,
and you'll need your strength.

The door closed. My eyes were full
of darkness. I sat still a long time,
holding my breath, not weeping,
breathing with a single fallen tear
passing through my restraint.
Then, I held my breath again.

I crawled around the room on my hands and knees, exploring the smooth stone floor, and the square room. My hands found the walls, and the men mortared together there. I wondered if any of them could see from their stone eyes. I wondered if anyone could bring them back from death. I had heard of a Bishop in Thrace that could pour holy water on cursed men, and cure their leprosy. I had heard of an Anchorite in Baghdad that spouted prayers to God that made flower petals pour from her cell. I wondered if praying to god could help these stone men. I knew no prayers but one. Please, God... Please, God... Please, God...

I got hungry again. I ate cherries until my stomach needed more room for food.

I considered leaving the room, and
considered the terrible monster
that would have tuned me into
stone telling me to stay here.
Feeling ill from the cherries, I used
a corner. I went to a different
corner to try and sleep. I knew I
would have restless nights, and I
would wake up nothing like how I
had fallen asleep. When I awoke,
I'd have to be careful not to fall
into my own mess.

I wondered if I'd be killed in the
morning, when the Architect Guild
came. I had assumed I would be
killed when I arrived, either as a
stone or eaten or strangled. I did
not expect this.

Eventually, I slept. Unlike the
ship, I was able to stretch out on
the stone ground. I pressed my ear
against the floor.

The stone men whispered to me of their endless dreams. When I slept I wandered the hills and valleys of the Palace's sleeping souls. A thousand love affairs, a thousand feasts, a thousand lullabies and a thousand nightmares all joined into one sound in my head, like a white hum. When I woke up, I knew exactly where I was. I was unable to forget all night long, even in sleep.

In Antioch, they said the Hashashan cannot walk these halls in peace with their holy herbs, and Sufis weep and weep if they are brought here. They say that King Basilisk is mad for all these sleeping stones infecting dreams.

I ran my hands along the floor that
had been planed down to flat from
a criminal's rocky flesh. I wept for
all these doomed ones, in the
walls. Architects were master
craftsmen of the fearful dead. They
found ways to make bodies
writhing in agony fit together as
close as bricks. They must have
studied their subjects closely to so
skillfully place these misshapen
bricks together like a concrete
quilt.

I wondered at the kind of soul that
could think of all these dead,
dreaming souls as bricks. I was
more afraid of them than King
Basilisk.

I ate more cherries.

I heard human footsteps in the
hall. I turned to face the sound of

footsteps. They stopped outside my door. I heard the door opening. I held my breath.

Are you still here, thief? A man's voice, just like a prison guard's: gruff, uncaring, impatient.

I said nothing.

King Basilisk said you were here. Don't make me come in there looking for you. The King is merciful. I am not. My name is Muzzenein. If you want to live, you'll speak up.

I let my breath go. Can't you see me?

Of course not. We wear blindfolds
in the palace. We wanted to give
the King a bell to wear around his
neck, but he would never allow
such an indignity. You're a woman,
then? I didn't expect that.

Are you going to kill me?

We should. We contracted with
Antioch and received payment for
your stoning. They're not supposed
to send us blind ones. Happens
now and then. Those Franj are a
sloppy bunch, and too rich for their
own good. They have taken your
city, but they have not taken up its
ways.

Please don't kill me, I whimpered.
I fell to my knees. Please don't...

We need all the help we can get in

the yard. Let's go, thief.

Rebecca, I said. My name is
Rebecca. I was crying.

He walked up to me. He placed a
hand on my head. Then, he found
my shoulder. He pulled at me,
roughly. It doesn't matter what
your name is if you can't work
hard.

I stood up. He bruised my arm
with his grip. He dragged me back
to the yard full of the stoned
criminals. Many men, and I
assumed they were all wearing
blindfolds like the one that led me
here. They bumped into each other
sometimes and cursed each other
for their blindfolds, and worked
hard here for the Architect Guild.
They hefted the stones onto

pallets. They were sorted by shape
and size, arranged by boys who
rang bells to announce the pallets
and the place. Men with arms
raised went on one pallet with a
high, keening bell. Collapsed into
fetal balls went on another, with a
doom-laden dark bell. Stoically
embracing stone their fate,
standing strong and proud for all
time, went on another, with
another sound entirely. Small men
went one place. Large men on
another. Women went to the same
pallet, with the smallest bell of all.
They were to be smoothed down
into long panels and formless
shapes to protect the populace
from the sight of so much naked
curves.

If Muzzenein was working, I never
noticed it. I overheard some of the
cursing directed towards the
leaders of the Architects, but I
could never hear it well enough to
make it out exactly. I do not expect

he was sweating in the yard beside
these men and me.

Any clothes or rags were piled in
the center of the yard to be burned.

I worked with the men, moving
heavy stones onto pallets. I wasn't
strong. I dropped legs, and heard
the crash when my side of a body
fell. I tripped on stones when I
didn't know where they were. I ran
into men that cursed and hit me
towards the right direction. I don't
know how all these men could
work so hard blindfolded, and find
the pallets, and all the bodies.

During a rest, the man who had
come to find me in the room gave
me a flask of watered-down wine.
He told me his name was
Muzzenein, the Third of the

Architects. He told me that King Basilisk desired my help in the garden when we were done in the yard. He would lead me there himself.

If I lived long enough, he said to me, I wouldn't need directions.

In the garden, the king urged me to pick more fruits. Blueberries, raspberries, strawberries, and all the fruits of late summer. Baskets were replaced with new baskets, and Muzzenein and the King ate the fruits I had harvested in silence.

King Basilisk asked Muzzenein to read books of faraway places. I listened when I could. From his voice, I know he read from behind a curtain. From the smell, I knew he needed a candle to see inside

the curtain, though we were in the
yard in full sunlight. I listened
while I worked. Snow-capped
peaks, and islands full of deadly
poisons, and strange festivals of
saints I had never known all were
read slowly from scrolls and books
I had never touched. I couldn't
imagine how anyone could read
words off a page, or how anyone
could remember all the pictures
and all the meanings of the
pictures. When Muzzenein read in
Greek or Latin, I couldn't
understand him, though I
recognized the sound of the Franj,
and Al-Arrabiya from the markets
of my native Antioch.

When evening twilight darkened
my eyes, and I had spent all day in
hard labor, I was too tired and sore
to think of far-off places. I had
stopped listening long ago. When I
was told to stop, I collapsed where

I fell.

I had been eating fruit the whole
time, while I worked, but I was
still hungry. I was still thirsty. I
was feeling sick to my stomach,
and needed something that wasn't
fruit to eat.

King Basilisk told Muzzenein to
take me to my room and give me
some bread. Muzzenein had to
wrap my arm over his shoulder
and carry me into the palace.

I didn't want to go back to my
room. I wanted somewhere soft to
sleep after all this work.

Muzzenein pushed me hard inside
a large door. He had not taken me
to my assigned room. He had
taken me to a chamber with a bed,

a chamber pot, and a bathtub full of hot water. He gave me a choice. He said there were not so many women inside King Basilisk's Palace, and not so many that would touch an Architect.

Of course I consented to him. I wanted to stay alive. I wanted to eat good food and sleep in a soft bed for one night. Mostly, I was afraid of what would happen if I refused him.

It wasn't so bad, with Muzzenein. I got to take a bath first, and sleep in a bed. He rubbed my sore muscles with oil and honey, while I ate from his own tray. He took his time rubbing my sore arms and back. All I had to do was hold still for him, because he knew I was tired.

He had a new dress for me in the morning, it felt smooth and cool on my skin. I had never worn cotton before. It may have been the finest thing I had ever touched in my life. Good cotton clothing was more valuable than gold.

In the morning, new criminals came on the ship, from a city I did not know. I lounged in bed with Muzzenein, pretending not to hear anything. The screams of the men were cut from the air as if with a knife. The new stones remained in the yard for one rainstorm. Muzzenein explained this to me. Fleas and lice and bedbugs clung to flesh and rags. However, if they remained attached to stones one rainstorm washed the parasites away. It rained here nearly every night so close to sea.

Other architects lived in the palace, but I never saw them or heard their footfalls. Muzzenein told me that he had never walked all the way from one end of the palace to the other. This sprawling palace grew to such great heights and distances. The world had an endless supply of new stones to feed the walls.

While I was picking fruits, I discovered what the king was doing with them. He made jams, preserves, and candies. He brought his latest batch to the garden to show to Muzzenein. They both sampled the jam, and discussed how it could be improved. More honey, perhaps. More pectin. Perhaps less. Perhaps the jars weren't clean enough. They offered none to me. I just picked fruit, quietly.

I lived that day. I lived another. I found my way from Muzzenein's room to the garden and to the yard without help. The King gave me a piece of candy to try. I told him it was the best thing I had ever eaten in my life. I was not lying.

What did you steal to be sent to me?

My king?

You know what I am asking. You were a thief. What did you steal?

Everything I could, my lord. I pretended to be a beggar, and I picked pockets. Nobody suspected the blind girl. Then, I pretended to be a chamber maid, and snuck into houses. I worked as good as anybody in the dark.

Muzzenein scoffed at me. I expected at least some kind of sad story about an orphan girl who could either steal or sell herself.

The King ran a hand across my cheek. Muzzenein, she is useful because she can steal, and because she can keep me company when you cannot. If she were truly incorrigible, we'd find all sorts of things in her pockets even now. You have not lost a hairbrush, or a shiny little ring?

She got caught, my friend. How useful could she be?

We will get caught, too, someday, Muzzenein. Some brave Franj or Marmluk or Turk will kill me as a

monster, and dedicate my death to
their faceless god. You'll be killed
for travelling with a monster. But,
before we do, we will see the world
beyond these walls. I think we
have enough jam to start. I have
received word from my sea
captains of Iberia, and jam prices
are very high. They'll be higher
when we get there in winter. They
only grow apples and vegetables in
the mountains. Their berries do
not make fine jams as ours do.

Now we should definitely kill her.
She'll tell the others.

The King ran a delicate claw down
my cheek. I was silent, and too
tired to scream.

Perhaps. Kill her if you think it
best, Muzzenein. But, do it
yourself and do it now, or don't do
it at all. Either way, stop talking
about it. You're scaring her.

The king pulled his claw from me.
He walked across his garden
without disrupting a single bush or
tree. He opened the door into the
palace. He closed it behind him.

I listened to Muzzenein breathing.
I held very still.

Not even insects survived the sight
of King Basilisk. No crickets or
buzzing flies filled the empty air.

Muzzenein held as still as I did. He
came no closer to me.

I broke the silence. Are you going
to...?

Of course not, he said. He grunted

at me.

I sold myself on the street too,
sometimes, I said. What was I
supposed to do - starve? Who
knows what diseases I carry inside
of me. I'd have killed if I had to. I
can think of men I wanted to kill. I
thought of him, threatening me
while eating the fruit I had picked
for him, while letting him pluck
me like a fruit in the dark. I bit my
tongue. I didn't want to threaten
him, because I didn't want to be
hit, or to die.

My father was an Architect, he
said. His voice was slow, now, like
the king's windy words. He
sounded tired when he spoke to
me. My grandfather was an
architect, too. My great-
grandfather was one of the first.
The King was not always the King.
Once, he was just a monster that

was tired of living alone. He found
a city that was tired of being
ignored by the cruel queen that
ruled it. Together, with the
architects, he built one of the
greatest cities in the world. The
Franj avoid our haunted walls.
The Hashishan go mad sneaking
through here with their spiritual
herbs and all the soulful stones.
Not even the Tartar Chiefs of the
Far East send their warriors here.
Many of your Franj believe us to
be the devil's kingdom on earth,
and they cannot muster the
strength to conquer us as easily as
they did Jerusalem or Antioch.
They fear the demons in the walls
more than the walls themselves.

Instead, they send us their sinners
as if sending them from God to
Hades. They pay us to take their
sinners. The King calls the stones
a merciful fate. He urges us to be

merciful, always. I will not kill
you. I wanted to scare you to keep
you quiet about what the king and
I want to do. Don't tell anyone
we're going to leave, and you can
come with us. Experienced thieves
are useful on the road, blind or
not, as the King said. I'm building
a special carriage for the King. Our
special ship is already completed
in the bay, waiting for us. He will
sneak away in the night, and I will
go with him, and we will travel all
over the world. We will see the
world together, and find a place
without all these terrible dreams
of fear and greed.

I heard the Architects footfalls.
Muzzenein walked towards me,
like stalking a rabbit. I tensed. I
readied to fight him. I lifted my
arms up to strike out.

He was not much stronger than

me, but he was strong enough to pull my face against his face. He was strong enough to kiss me.

Of course I let him. What choice did I have? I stumbled into this gruesome cathedral in chains. I fell at the gargoyle's feet. I had to accept the terms of my unconditional surrender.

When Muzzenein was kissing me, I considered strangling him in his sleep once the basilisk has us out on the road, and then I could escape into the night in a crowded city. Even this idea was distant. I had never killed anyone. I had never wanted to, really, though I wouldn't have minded if someone had died. I wouldn't mind at all if Muzzenein died.

I prayed with the only words of
prayer I knew.

Please, God... Please, God...
Please, God...

I don't know what I was begging
for, or what I would have done
with it were heaven to give
something to me.

Night descended. The sea storm
gathered with damp air and wind.
I imagined everyone was blind in
the moonless, clouded darkness. As
I thought of this, lightning flashed
through the darkness of my eyes. I
wondered if we would truly remain
here, in darkness. I wondered if
the rain would come and wake up
the Architect when the wind
chilled him to the bone.

Lady or the Tiger, Death Mask and Eulogy,

and Other Re-Imaginings

I slipped Muzzenein's mask from his face. I threw it into the garden, where rain would turn all this soft earth to mud.

I don't know if I really wanted to kill Muzzenein. I wanted to scare him. I wanted to hurt him. I wanted to deserve my fate.

THE LADY OR THE TIGER

*Re-imagined from a tale by Frank
Stockton, 1882*

Many years ago, when I was a boy
of only ten, I was in a terrible
crash on the cliffs south of Io
Town, where nights are a deep
tundra freeze and afternoons are
as hot as a summer on the long
plains. Even now, I close my eyes
and I can still see Sheila's face just
before she was crushed under two
thick layers of plasteel.

I had watched her half of the flyer

cracking away from mine, and rolling on top of her.

And collapsing.

On top of her.

Her scream disappeared from the icy air so fast, the only way I knew it had been real was the echo of it, down the canyons, where a small avalanche threw rocks and snow down to the stream.

I tried to free her, but my brother, Jiri, stopped me because the freeze would preserve her until we could dig her out during the warm day, and we had to make our shelter before we froze to death. We had our survival to worry about. We could save her in the morning.

So that's what we did.

We were in our shelter. We were warm, and mostly safe enough. Jiri had told me to try to get some sleep.

I couldn't sleep because I was thinking about her. I tried to remember the songs she sang over me while I swam in the river, or the special way she had of preparing sandwiches for me, with the crusts cut off and the sauce on both sides. Then, all I could think of was the explosion, the fall, the screaming, and the crushing sound of the plasteel, and blood in the snow from when my brother had used flaming wreckage to burn the stumps shut at his lost fingers.

The only thing I could think of to take my mind off of Sheila, and the crash, was asking my brother about Guj Sarwar, the tiger on the back of the great and mighty lizard, Samarkand. When I was a boy, I didn't understand why it was the only other thing I could think about, like something was on the tip of my tongue.

And, Jiri knew everything there was to know about the wastes of the far west, the lizards, and the tigers. He was fifteen years old. Next year, he'd be driving cattle up the highway to Io Town in a flyer all by himself. I was only ten. I didn't even have my own computer terminal yet. I had to share his when he wasn't using it. Everything I knew about the wastes had been from the computer, and from Jiri.

"On the wastes, Simsa," said my brother, "you can't walk on the ground. The sand is all quicksand. It sucks you up and swallows you. You have to ride on the back of giant lizards as big as walking mountains. There're only twenty-five lizards. They have names."

"Are there plants on the wastes?"

"Of course there're plants, Simsa. There're plants everywhere; even out here on the high canyons, clover grows, and molds line the cliff walls. The lizards of the wastes eat the floating molds and large bushes that grow on top of the quicksand like forests of soap scum. The people keep their houses on the back ridges because the constant up-and-down of the head drives you nuts when the lizard's feeding."

"How do they survive there?"

"People live in huts, on the lizards.
They grow blood wheat. They mine
for lizard flesh, but they have to be
careful not to cut a vein, or the
beast will bleed like crazy. They
trade, like we do at the station."

It was sixty below freezing outside
by now. The tent skin radiated
enough heat to keep us warm. The
dead grass and snow blowing
around outside wouldn't penetrate
past the magnets that held the flap
shut.

My brother had wrapped his
bloodied, burned hand in part of
his shirt. He had lost two fingers
in the crash, and had burned them

mostly shut. The wound extended
up his palm. It still bled a little,
now and then. Jiri had gotten his
smoke-smelling blood on the
handles of our hot mugs of
chocolate milk.

I leaned back. I closed my eyes.
"What about the tigers?"

"There's only one tiger left. And,
he's not really a tiger," he said.
"Not really"

"At school, I heard Frankie say
there was a lizard that had
nothing but tigers."

"Frankie's so dumb; he wouldn't
know which end of the battery to
shove up his own ass."

I laughed. "That's what Frankie said to me about the tigers," I said. "He said there was a lizard with only tigers on it."

"Well, don't believe everything you hear. There's only one tiger left. One. He's not even really a tiger. He just has a tiger-like head. He lives on Samarkand, the biggest, oldest lizard in all the wastes. You know Samarkand because his legs are covered in scars. Nobody knows why. A scientist said the scars were from when Samarkand tried to walk out of the waste. Lizards don't leave the waste, though—not ever. They can't survive out of the quicksand. Their feet only work right in the wastes."

The winds outside swelled. Sand splattered the side of the tent. Both of us grabbed for the edge of our tent. We waited until the gust passed. When it had, my brother lay his sleeping pad over the edge, right up against the heat.

"Simsa," he said. "Try to get some sleep. We'll have a million things to do in the morning."

"Where do you think Samarkand's scars came from?"

He rolled over onto his side. He looked at me, lying in the middle of our little tent. "I think he got in a fight with another lizard. And, I think he won. I think that's why there aren't any more lizards with scars. The other lizards give Samarkand a wide berth along the wastes. They see him walking over the horizon, they turn away."
Then, because he was too tired to speak anymore, he said, "Go to

sleep, Simsa."

I sat in the dark. I watched Jiri sweat, pressed against the heated tent skin, breathing gently. I drank hot chocolate. I hugged my legs. I thought about tomorrow, and what we'd have to do for Sheila, and for ourselves.

~~~

I had known everything before my brother told me, but I didn't want him to know that. Guj Sarwar, currently living on Samarkand, was the only survivor of the battle on the space elevator. He was part of the isolationist faction that had almost destroyed the Ansible. The tigers had climbed up the outside of the elevator at Io Town, with nano-particle scimitars strapped to their backs. They knew the

Parliament would send electromagnetic pulses along the outside to stop anyone from climbing up. The fighters had to make their hands sharp claws to grip, even when the pulses tried to throw their hands and feet off. They had to make their bodies capable of surviving the climb into the thermosphere. They had to grow fur, and alter their noses and mouths to seal the flammable oxygen blends against the electomagnetic defenses. They couldn't count on just goggles. They traded eyes with cave cats. They needed to see in low light to get to the Mesosphere in the dark.

There's only one tiger left after the battle. He's been hiding out on the head of Samarkand for twelve years. Everyone who went after him got sliced to ribbons, or dumped into the wastes. These days, he's just left alone. He can't speak anymore. Tiger mouths don't speak except in growls and roars.

He can't type messages into
computer terminals, either. His fur
interrupts EM radiation too much
to get him anywhere near a
terminal without shorting it out.
His claws are no good at holding a
stylus, or a pen. He can only carve
burning letters with his deadly
scimitar, which isn't an effective
method of communication when
most things would be burned and
eaten into ash by the nanites.

He lives isolated from mankind
forever after losing the war; he
destroyed himself to fight. Yet, for
some reason known only to him, he
refuses to turn himself in or
commit honorable suicide.

His army of tigers had failed. The
Ansible was built. The ships come
and go, trading and trading. By
the time I was old enough to notice

a world outside the ranch, the war
that had claimed Guj Sarwar's
humanity, and all the brave
Isolationists that had become
tigers and died on Io Town's space
elevator, was already mostly
forgotten.

These days, Guj Sarwar was
stalking the blood wheat fields in
the dark, stealing sausage and
chasing down the birds that are
native to the thickets on the back
of the beast. He left people alone
as long as they left him alone.

~~~

In the morning, Jiri flipped the
heating skin off. We were both
sweating. It was better than
freezing. We had to wait in our
tent and change into dry clothes. If
we stepped outside with any damp

on us before the sun had burned off all the snow, we might freeze to death.

We drank the last of our chocolate milk. It wasn't going to keep, anyway, when the refrigeration unit would be otherwise in use.

When we were dry, we wrapped ourselves in clean, dry clothes and stepped outside. We had a lot of cutting to do. Sheila's body was trapped under at least two layers of plasteel.

She'd never be the same again, but a clone of her with whatever memories survived would be better than losing her forever. The deep chill of the night would have preserved almost everything. The afternoons got too warm, though.

The day's weather would heat up rapidly, melt the snow down into underground aquifers. By mid-afternoon the winds would change and the weather would quickly turn into a harsh chill, snow falling everywhere. We had to get her out before the heat rotted her brain synapses.

That wasn't all we had to do. We were out of water. As soon as noon passed, and the sun turned away from our cliffside, the chill would be back, and we'd have to be prepared in our tent for another long night, waiting for rescue. We needed water to do that, or we'd die of thirst long before we had ever starved.

We were, fortunately, crashed on a cliff that overlooked a mountain stream deep below. The stream was frozen now, but by mid-morning it would flow cold and clean.

As soon as our tent's registered a safe outdoor temperature, we went to Sheila. Jiri had the tools.

"Do you think you can get us some water, Simsa?"

I shook my head. "Sheila."

"I can get Sheila."

"I want to be sure," I said. I choked up.

"Whiny baby... Fine. You do the cutting." He pulled the hand torch

J. M. McDermott

from our toolkit.

"Be careful, though. Don't heat her body up."

I took the torch. I toggled a couple of the switches. I pulled at the trigger. Nothing happened.

My brother snatched it from my hands. "Don't know how, do you?"

I looked at where we knew Sheila was, under the rubble. "I don't want to leave her."

My brother took a deep breath. "Simsa..."

I started to cry.

282

"Fine. Just… Try not to get in my way."

He adjusted the nozzles and switches on the little torch. He touched the plasteel. The metal was slow to cut through. It was freezing cold. I watched my brother work.

I looked around the camp for something I could do. We had our tent lashed down tightly. We had a couple boxes of supplies–another toolkit, some emergency rations–lashed down next to the tent. Jiri had the larger toolkit out, with the torch, the anchor and the repel line. The ship's refrigeration unit had ejected, with food and milk, near the top of the pile of rubble, batteries still intact. It was better than emergency rations. When we dug Sheila out, it would keep her

head frozen through the warm
afternoons.

I wondered if I shouldn't watch for
snow lizards, or pterodactyls, or
other scavengers after easy blood.

Jiri needed help pulling the first
layer off. I took one end, and he
took the other. He could barely
grip anything with his two missing
fingers and the cut up his palm.
The stumps started to bleed again.
He didn't say anything. He just
tightened the bandage until it
stopped.

The next layer was going to be
harder, because it was the outer
shell of the flyer. It was still cold
enough below the plasteel, so we
knew Sheila would still be frozen.

Jiri took a long drink of our last
quart of milk. "Simsa, what else

did that poop-for-brains Frankie
tell you about the tiger of
Samarkand?"

"He told me... I don't know."

"Well, there were many tigers.
Hundreds of them. They knew
they would never be able to stop
the Ansible, or shut down Io
Town's space elevator."

"Why'd they want to do that?" I
said. "It's stupid."

"They were idealists—
uncompromising. They had to try.
They were fools, of course. They
killed people. No ideals are worth
killing people. They were
terrorists. Only idiots are

terrorists. If Frankie had been around during that time, he would be just the poop-for-brains that would join them."

"What were they so worried about, anyway? Why do they hate the Ansible and the space elevator?"

"Minerals, carbon, and the planet. You know, our cattle grow here on grass and wheat that we grow on-world. They go to Io Station to be taken off-world, into space, for merchants all over the galaxy."

"Yeah."

"Well, they carry part of the planet with them. Carbon, and vitamins, and little bits and pieces of molecules that we cannot bring back. In exchange, do you know what we get?"

"Money?"

"Plastic. Plasteel. Silicates.
Machines made of these things.
That refrigerator. This ship.
Things that don't make life."

"Frankie doesn't know anything
about that."

"Of course not. Anyway, they were
being stupid. We can just trade for
things later then bring back what
we need. It's all stupid."

I knew this already. I had seen the
videos. The protests were all over
the world for a while, before the

Ansible was built, before I was born. I had watched them on Jiri's computer, late at night.

We had to hurry to get through the next layer before the freeze wore off with the direct sun on the plasteel shell. We didn't have much time.

About halfway through the side of the wall, Jiri stopped trying to cut it all. He looked up at the sun. It wasn't mid-morning yet, but it was close to it. He took a deep breath. He started to focus on just one part, near the top, where the hand tool's X-Ray gave a readout of Sheila's head below the plasteel. Jiri cut just there, hurriedly.

"What are you doing?" I said. "You're doing it wrong."

"Simsa, go get water," he said. "I'll be done when you get back."

"I'm not leaving her."

"Simsa, listen, you don't want to be here when I cut through the second wall. It's not going to be pretty."

"I don't care," I said. "I won't leave her."

"It's not that, Simsa," he said. "It's... Look, we're almost out of time. We just need to preserve her head. It's all we can fit in the refrigeration unit, anyway."

"Oh," I said. I closed my eyes. I

was crying, again. "Oh."

He was right.

I turned away.

"You know how to do this?" I said. "I mean, you know exactly what you're doing, and you won't hurt her?"

He peeled away a strip of plasteel. "She's going to be fine," he said. "She'll walk funny a few days, then she'll be fine. She'll remember everything but the crash. It'll be like nothing happened. I promise. Go get some water, Simsa. I'll be done when you get back."

"Okay," I said.

I gathered the ropes and canteens.
I listened to the sound of the
plasteel melting off in strips,
tossed aside in a rush.

The rocks were craggy and jagged.
I walked down the mountain, and
imagined I was climbing down the
ridges of a lizard in the wastes. I
imagined I was a tiger, sneaking
down the neck of Samarkand in
the night to steal crops and
vandalize the things from off
world.

At the bottom of the cliff, the
stream was slow and thin. I
couldn't easily get water inside the
canteens. I used my hands to cup
water, and pour it in. Then, I
dropped the purifier pills into the
full canteens and capped them

shut. It took time. I had plenty of time. I didn't want to be on the top of the cliff until my brother was done and had covered up the mess.

A pack of tundra lizards splashed over the rocks in the stream. They were about as big as my father's boots. They only had one, primitive eye. They swayed from side-to-side to single me out against the rocks. I frowned at them. "Go away," I said.

Tongues flicked in the air. These scavengers had smelled the blood on me.

I stood up. I waved my hands around. They backed away. "Go away!" I shouted. My voice echoed up the canyon. The lizards scattered into the porous cliffside at the water's edge.

I gasped and cowered at the walls

around me. Had I caused an avalanche?

Tiny rocks dribbled down, nothing more. Jiri would be mad at me for yelling. I should have known better. I was a rancher's son, and this was my planet. I should have thrown stones at the lizards. They're scavengers, hunting for dead pterodactyls and bugs, and never interested in a struggle.

I took my time on the way up, thinking about what I'd say to my brother about my shout. I left the rope pull on its lowest setting. It was safest at a slow setting, up the cliff, especially after that shout.

I hoped my brother had placed some kind of tarp or cloth or bit of abandoned steel over the body. I hoped he wouldn't yell at me for shouting.

Day heat broke. I felt the air bite through my clothes. Snow began to fall. It was going to be another freezing night, and rescue hadn't found our crash site yet. They might not find us for another day or two. Io Town wouldn't notice one ranch flyer out of the five we flew up to the different trading sites. Even our men would empty the cargo trailer and turn home. Our parents would only notice when our flyer didn't come home on schedule. They might try to call and leave a message, but our communicators had been lost in the crash. It might be days before they suspected anything, and even more days until they found us.

The rope pulled me up without any effort. I just walked up the wall of the cliff, slowly and carefully.

Calmness washed over me, as I
neared the top. I believed that
everything was going to be fine. In
a week, we'd all be back home at
the ranch, sitting around the
kitchen table eating ice cream and
nothing would be different.

I crawled over the lip of the cliff
and climbed to the top on hands
and knees. I looked up, to my
brother.

Jiri had collapsed face down on top
of the final wall of plasteel. Beetles
had found his pooled blood, at his
wounded hand, and buzzed around
it, slurping it up and feasting on it,
laying eggs in the finger stumps.

I vomited.

Then, I stood up. I dropped the
canteens. I yanked the rope loose
and away from my waist.

I ran to him, and to her.

My brother had slipped in her
blood with the lathe in his hand.
He had accidentally cut a new part
of his wounded hand with it, and
that had opened the whole wound
where his fingers were missing, up
onto his palm. He had cut through
most of her head when he had
blacked out from blood loss. He
was so close to saving her that he
hadn't stopped in time to save
himself. I pulled him back from the
wreckage.

I saw Sheila's face.

Lady or the Tiger, Death Mask and Eulogy,

and Other Re-Imaginings

Her beautiful face was ruined. It was smashed. It was sticky, partially-frozen blood. It wasn't Sheila. It wasn't the woman who had kissed me twice because I was her favorite, or sung songs while she watched me swimming, or had always pretended to need my help with jars. This face was some other thing–some awful thing, all bloody and mangled and covered in scavenging beetles.

My brother's body was still warm. He wasn't breathing. He had no pulse.

Her head was warming in direct sunlight, losing more synaptic connections every moment spent in the afternoon heat that muddied the bloody ice frost around what was left of her hair.

I grabbed the hand torch. I
fumbled with it until I got it to
ignite.

I only had the one refrigeration
unit.

It was only big enough for one
head.

Do I save the lady, or the tiger?

~~~

I called my brother a tiger, because
I knew he was the one responsible,
even then, when I was just a boy.
Deep down inside, I knew. I knew
all about Guj Sarwar on the back

of Samarkand before I'd asked my brother anything. I had read it from my brother's page history on the computer we shared at home. I had read the same tracts and stories and propaganda. I had seen the same videos. My brother didn't know that.

We had been flying cattle to our family holding pens at the foot of the Io Town space elevator to ship off-world, where their minerals and carbons and life-giving things would be lost to this world. The cattle were gone, now.

Sheila had ejected the cattle in their cargo trailer when trouble had started. They weren't awake to scream. They fell. They crashed. Already the lizards and pterodactyls of the high plains would have picked the bones of the cattle clean to the bone.

I had been sitting next to Sheila in
the cockpit, strapped in. My
brother was behind me. I looked up
at her, beautiful and wild, a
woman so much older than me, a
child, and I loved her terribly. She
was terrified. She was shouting
and bouncing in her seat and
praying and pushing buttons and
looking at me and at my brother
and back at her dials.

And my brother, I knew, had
caused this.

A few cans of condensed air,
hidden in the cargo stabilizers,
pressurized in flight when the
vessel crossed above the
troposphere. They exploded,
knocking the stabilizers off the
side of the cargo container. Guj

Sarwar taught that to his followers before they lost their humanity and embraced more violent actions. A good pilot could dump the cargo and fly home safely.

Sheila, the woman I loved, was not a good pilot. She was an adequate pilot. She was only flying cargo because my father, and all his men, were already flying cargo. It was a large shipment. Sheila usually didn't fly. She had asked us to come with her to keep her company. When the stabilizers broke, she didn't dump the cargo fast enough. The destabilized cargo had jackknifed and slammed against her side of the ship. She'd been stunned for a few moments too long before Jiri had shouted at her to dump the cargo. Then we'd been falling, falling, falling...

My brother, the Isolationist. The
tiger.

I had the cutting tool in my hand.

My brother, even after what he'd
done, had never meant to kill
anyone. Even at ten years old, I,
too, could sense the romance of the
tiger of Samarkand, and the
Isolationists. Sheila was just an
employee who cleaned our houses,
watched over the children, and
flew my brother and me to market
when we were due for a treat. And,
just as importantly, I loved her as
only a ten-year-old could love. She
was his victim. She never deserved
this.

Sheila. My beautiful lady.

I tightened my grip on the hand

torch. I could not hesitate. Each moment spent deciding was another memory lost forever.

Did I save the lady or the tiger?

Whom should I have saved?

I am a man, now, with a ranch of my own on Samarkand's back. I will always wonder if I made the right choice.

ABOUT THE AUTHOR

J M McDermott is a robot fueled by
literature, vegetables, and caffeine. He
lives in San Antonio, TX, where he stands
on street corners and shouts at passing
cars about the future.

He holds a BA in Creative Writing from
the University of Houston, and an MFA in
Popular Fiction from the Stonecoast
Program of the University of Southern
Maine.

His other books include *Never Knew
Another, Last Dragon, When We Were
Executioners, Maze, Disintegration
Visions,* and *Women and Monsters.*

Made in the USA
Middletown, DE
17 February 2020